HOME

Blue Solace, Book 2
ANGELA DAWN STATEN

~~
Copyright © 2015 by Angela Dawn Staten
All rights reserved, including the right of reproduction in whole or in part in any form.
https://angeladawnsworld.wordpress.com

First published in December 2015. Available from Amazon.com, CreateSpace.com, and other retail outlets 2016. Scripture quotations are taken from the Holman Christian Standard Bible. Copyright 2003 by Holman Bible Publishers. Used by permission.

Cover: Drop Dead Designs ©2017

The characters and events portrayed in this book are fictitious.

Home: a novel / by Angela Dawn Staten.
Summary: The survivors from the planned zombie outbreak must now face the Demons and other supernatural beings… The new Leader of the Vampires has followed the Hunters to Tennessee and is working with unexpected allies… And Lucas Kale must find a way to deal with the loss of someone close to him… A death he blames himself for…
~~

Again, this is for my mom Mary. And my English teacher Frankye Holmes. She asked me a ton of questions, but this one stands out the most. "Have you considered a future in writing?"
My answer was no.
~~~

CONTENTS

Prologue	1
1. As Told From	3
2. Flash me Back	27
3. Again, Please	55
4. The Beginning of the Sword	67
5. Cracks	83
6. South Carolina	105
7. King Eben	135
8. July	147
9. What Happened In August	163
10. Raven's Thunder	173
11. October	197
12. Day of the Dead	221
Epilogue	249 |//
About the Author	

Whatever happens, do not lose hold of the two main ropes of life—hope and faith.

Prologue

Tennessee

I PULL THE curtain back from my bedroom window and stare out across the lawn. At first the moonlight throws me off and I just see my reflection; my disheveled blonde hair and lost hazel eyes. I don't even want to know what the rest of me looks like. I stare out, letting my eyes adjust to my Chevy Biscayne parked in the grass. My car had taken a serious beating; the windows smashed out—and that's not the worst of it. The car is broken. Damaged. But the memories of HER aren't—no, I don't think anything could ever alter those.

I let the curtain fall from my fingertips, and I don't know how long I stand there; just staring at the plain white and blue pattern. After zoning out, I stride across my room and sit down at my desk. My bloodshot eyes feel as though they are going to pop out of my head as I stare wildly at the journal and ballpoint pen my Uncle Joe gave me earlier today like they're aliens about to take me to Hell. I don't know what else to do; I've tried everything I can possibly think of but nothing has killed the agony inside of me—not even punching my mirror this morning. I finally admit I have nothing to lose and swoop up the pen. I flip the leather journal open and begin; refraining from just ripping the page with the pen's tip until there's nothing left.

October 5

The girl—woman—whom I have spent the last few months with, who saved me and Leon and the world from... She is gone. Raven is dead. Her funeral was today. And I feel as lost and lonely as ever.

In fact, I wish I had never met Raven.
—Lucas Kale

Chapter 1
As Told From

Concordia, Kansas. About five months earlier.
(May)

BLAYNE VANDOR

BLAYNE LAID sprawled out on a cave rock with two necklaces placed next to his head; one with a red ruby, the other a violet unicorn. Avy Sinanna, close by on another large rock, turned over on his side with his back to him. Avy was his new mentor and leader of the Vampires since Kronos was cleverly killed by Raven and the Shadow Lana. Blayne watched the small flames from the torches as they continued to play an inaudible melody. His brown eyes became heavy. The sun was out. Blayne didn't know how he knew this but he did. His eyes closed shut; not bothering to put up a fight. It was time to rest.

"Hello, Boys."

Blayne jerked upright, a moment of sheer panic jolted through him. But it quickly subsided. Before him stood the blue-haired girl he met for the first time last night when his Vampire sister had been undead. But now Amaterasu was the true dead; *God's true dead*, as Bram Stoker called it his novel *Dracula* Blayne recalled.

Avy stood in between him and the sixteen-year-old-looking girl. "Silhou," he said bowing his head. Blayne had seen several bow to his last mentor but this was different. Blayne didn't know why she held some kind of unspoken authority over them, a kind of superiority that went beyond Avy's leadership, but he sure as heck didn't feel like *bowing* to her. He didn't bow when he first met her, and he partially blamed her for Amaterasu's death. If Kronos and Avy held the leadership position over him and the other Vampires, what made this Silhou so special? And *blue* hair? Not for him.

"Raven's," the pixie-haired girl said to Avy and tossed what looked to be unlabeled DVD's to the dirt floor…"Take care it."

"What are those? Who are you? *Exactly*?" Blayne demanded some answers. He suddenly felt wicked power emanating from the girl; coal black fangs flicked over her other teeth and instantly Blayne knew he had crossed some sort of boundary. He had never seen Vampire fangs of that nature.

Silhou played with the silvery trimmings of her blue, silky cape and laughed at Blayne as if he was the dumbest person in class. Her derisive laughs echoed off the cave walls, bounced around in his head, and ignited his temper quicker than the flick of a cigarette lighter. "Children," she said with an underlying insult; which Blayne instantly picked up on and his brow furrowed and his nostrils flared. "I'm not a child!" Before the aggravated tone in his voice had time to echo back to him, Blayne was pinned against the rock wall; feet elevated off the cave floor, and water heavily dripped down from up above and through his brunette hair due to the current damage done to the wall.

Avy Sinanna squeezed his neck so hard Blayne thought he was going to burst like a balloon. Blayne didn't need oxygen to survive, but he did need his throat, and the older Vampire could easily end his existence. "Avy…" he pleaded looking down at his mentor.

"Trust me. You want my threats more than you want hers," Avy warned him. Avy's reaction wasn't something the Novice expected; this was the first time he witnessed the Vampire became even remotely angry. "Now apologize," he demanded and loosened his grip around the recently born Vampire. Blayne, frightened and embarrassed, sincerely apologized. The elder Vampire let go of him and Blayne landed on his feet. He massaged his sore throat. Judging by the pain, Blayne was pretty sure Avy left handprints.

Smirking, the caped girl walked over to the torches burning along the wall; her hair nearly looked black in the small amount of light. She stopped in front of the wall and looked at Blayne. "What is it you wish to ask?" How did she know something was on his mind? Blayne was fairly certain he gave no indications of such things. He wanted to ask her what she was but decided not to. "Avy said certain names are important. I don't understand. In the stories wasn't a son of Kronos supposed to dethrone him?"

"A mortal's tale," Avy smirked.

"What's the real story?" Blayne asked inquisitively.

"This one," Silhou stated, and Blayne Vandor was aghast when she walked through the hard cave wall and disappeared like a ghost. While the water heavily poured down the giant crack in the cave's ceiling, all he could see was the reflection of his brown hair and Vampire-Novice eyes, standing there with a horrified expression on his young face.

Hastings, Nebraska
(May)

The Demon—the primary owner of the body since the real Mrs. Queen was tricked into giving it up—looked at the woman's bare skin in the mirror. The intestines were where they should be; the giant hole in the woman's stomach had mostly repaired from the gunshot injury that she was forced to inflict upon herself, making it easy for the Demon to get inside her body and control it—possess it.

When the bloody baseball-sized hole in the woman's lower abdomen finally closed over, completely healed by the demonic powers, Mrs. Queen—possessed— picked up the flower printed shirt only a mother would wear. She pushed her head through the hole and pulled it down over her bra and the healed shotgun wound. The Demon grinned at the reflection in the mirror, and the woman's eyes turned black and veins the color of tar ran through the white parts of her eyes. "Now all I need is for that daughter of yours to come home," Mrs. Queen winked.

* * *

October 5
Present Day
   (Lucas Kale reads from Lana's diary)

May 11

"Where in the hell have you been?"

Loki and I stopped at the bottom of the steps and looked up at her mother as she stormed out of my friend's big old-fashioned house. The door slammed hard behind the woman. "Mom?" I heard shock in Loki's voice; not shock from the woman's lack of concern for her child's well-being—which certainly wasn't anything new. But from the shear fact the woman was ALIVE. In that moment it dawned on me that Loki might have a death wish with her mother's name on it.

I was told about Leon's vision of Loki; how he saw her being eaten by her shameless mom. But then Loki left with me and Cole to find the woman from Leon's vision—Raven. It seems that Loki's absence here was what kept the drunk woman alive. Go figure.

"Answer me!" she yelled. I could easily see that she hadn't showered for DAYS. Her extremely oily and matted down

blonde hair reflected off the sun as she took a step down from the porch and into the light. Her hair is nothing like Loki's pretty curly hair.

I was a little disturbed by her mom. I never had high expectations of the woman, but I guess I thought a zombie apocalypse would have changed her somehow. NOPE!!!

"Mom, don't you remember what happened?" Loki asked.

"I remember drinking too much and having a bad trip. Meanwhile, while you were off gallivanting someone stole our guns!" The hung-over woman blinked away the yellow sunlight from her eyes, and spotted the gun in Loki's hand. "Get inside!" She gritted out through badly stained teeth. That was my cue to leave. "I'll see you later," I hugged Loki good-bye and quickly turned away. I don't know why Loki's mom was upset, but I knew I had to get away from the woman before I did something that I couldn't take back. And since I had accompanied Loki to her house, I figured it was time this Shadow went home to her own mother.

I missed my mom so much. Before I knew it I was across the yard, up the hill, and through the flat field that leads to my backyard. "Mom please be okay. Please be alive. Run. Run. Run," I screamed silently to myself as worry and excitement from the thought of her being alive all piqued inside of me. I blazed up the front steps and across our black deck. After I flung open the front doors I paused just inside the house. Silence. It was dark and the air was kind of stuffy. Was this a good thing? I wondered.

"Lana? Sweetie is that you?"

I instantly let the air out that I had been holding in. Relieved, I turned left into the kitchen and then immediately right entering our dining room. The dining table was set with cups, plates, forks, and even napkins. I saw that chicken was the main course. And at the far side of the table sat my wonderful mother! "Mom!" I ran to her. She placed her fork on the plate and stood up smiling. I immediately threw my arms around her. Our hair matches right down to every black root, but the smell of hers brought me back to a different time. A safe time. And for a moment it was okay. Everything was okay. I was back in Hastings and for the most part I'm okay.

"I was so worried about you," my mom confessed while she patted my nappy hair. I couldn't wait to shower and feel somewhat normal again. *"Do you remember what happened?"* I asked her.

"Of course, dear. How could I not?"

I told her that on our way back here Loki and I came across some people who were never bit, yet they seemed to have forgotten anyway. Like some sort of mental thing... Like the insanity of it all just drove them to forget; a sort of volunteer amnesia.

"You and Loki? Where's Cole?" She asked.

And there it was. My green eyes instantly moistened at the mentioning of his name. *"I-I-I. Mom, I killed him."* The words felt weird coming from my tongue, and my mother's grip tightened around me; hugging me. *"Oh sweetie, I'm so sorry. Sit. It will do you good to eat something."* My mom's warm eyes looked back at me caringly as her warm grip loosened. *"We can talk about it if you want..."*

(Got to go)
L. Queen

I moved to the bed sometime around the middle of Lana's entry. I close her diary and let it rest against my chest. On some level I knew I wasn't the only one who lost someone. But reading her words... Before, I never saw how reading Lana's and the others' thoughts was going to help me cope, but they sure seemed to think it would make a difference. I find it odd that this process is supposed to fix me because right now it's really killing me.

Her last sentence is imprinted in mind and I vividly see it like it's written on the wall; *we can talk about it if you want...* "Well, I don't. In fact, I don't want to talk at all. We've been through this, Leon," I remember telling my cousin in the car while the wind violently blew through the window in the back that had been busted out by a zombie. A zombie that had busted through and killed Kimberly. Her brother was the first zombie; transformed by the Vampire Kronos, but created by *the* one and only Satan.

"But we just left her there," whinny Leon protested next to me from the passenger seat while I steered our Chevy Biscayne around some stuff piled up on the interstate.

"We did our job." I reminded him.

"I don't see how you can be so callous?"

"Okay. That's it."

"What?"

I smile and shake my head; remembering back to what I did.

"Your turn." I pulled the car over on the side of

the interstate. "Apparently this is share-Leon's-feelings-time and if I have to listen I want to do it with my eyes closed," I told him and opened my door and got out. I heard him sigh. He was annoyed I could tell. I stopped at the front of the car and waited for his slow-moving butt. "How can you treat this like it's another job?" Leon asked after he finally got out of my way.

"Because it was." I handed my little cousin the keys and he tried staring me down with his lame blue eyes; expecting a real answer. "What about the Demons that now exist because she technically died, Luke?"

"We can start with the bastards in Tennessee," I said lurching inside the car and quickly shutting the door. *Wasn't it just another job?* I only asked myself; even though I knew it was much more and I couldn't admit it. Leon shook his head and sighed again before getting behind the steering wheel. "Are you seriously telling me you're not the least bit worried about her?"

"She told us to go. I'm sure Raven's fine. Now stop talking"—I reclined the seat all the way back—"I'm trying to sleep here."

"Unbelievable," Leon shook his head again and turned the ignition over. The sun was setting as we continued onto I-70 East. We passed by a sign that said *Illinois*. And I clearly remember saying, "I'm gonna sleep so good."

I guess that was just the beginning of my douchebag attitude when it came to Raven. Or maybe it was the day I met her—when she spilled coffee on me and called me a douche. Even though

I miss her that was still the best moment of my life. Lana's diary rising up and down on my chest while I breathe brings me back here, to the present, where I'm now twenty-five and I need to read a teenager's diary to make myself feel better. How pathetic. I decide to let sleep consume me. The last several days have been long, especially today with Raven's funeral…

* * *

(The past)
May 11
Concordia, Kansas

RAVEN & CRICKET

They are dead. Sheba. Ganesha. Jet. I will never see their faces again. Never hear their laughs. They will never be by my side fighting the fight against evil. I will never say good morning to the three of them. I will never tell them goodnight. Jet and I will never make Ganesha, Sheba, and Cricket breakfast, lunch, or dinner.

There is no Jet and I.

He's gone. The Werewolf who has been by my side for centuries, the man who was supposed to be in my life for eternity is dead. He doesn't exist.

They don't exist.

Raven heard debris being shuffled about behind her and she quickly blinked back to her spot on the grass. Mozart uncurled himself from his ball position as he laid beside her feet. Raven smiled at him. He was so big, yet he could curl his fluffy self into such a small ball. He laid on his back and fully stretched; his front and back paws sticking up in opposite directions, his lean stomach fully extended. Cricket sat down beside them and rubbed the Husky's belly. Cricket's dark hand moved in circles, and up and down through the dog's white fur. It brought a tiny smile to Raven's face. Moments of joy, no matter how big or small, were few and far in between today. When he was finished the dog flopped over on his side; ready to nod off again. Cricket and Raven could tell he was tired. All three of them were beyond exhausted.

Cricket was used to fighting Vampires—he was a Shadow, but he wasn't used to being in love with a Shadow. Or anyone really. That was just as new to him as was the universe lying to him. Cricket believed his friends, the Werewolf and his Raven, were supposed to be alive until the end of time, but the Vampires murdered Jet. And as he continued to sit beside Raven on the lawn out in front of what was left of their American home, Cricket knew that although Raven was alive something had died inside of his friend. He knew there was nothing he could do for her.

Raven found out the antidote for curing the infected humans—zombies—was her blood; she was half-human and half-Vampire. The Vampires used to her call her a Goddess, but now she was all human and she felt nothing like a Goddess. Somewhere between everyone going their separate ways and her siting on the lawn—for hours—the sun had begun to set. Giant fluffy clouds of orange with bright yellow popping out around the edges brought about the end to another day.

"Sheba would say, 'Yeah, sunset. There will be another one tomorrow.' Ganesha would pass me the bong," Raven smiled at the idea, and Cricket laughed a little. "Jet would…he…" She couldn't do it. She couldn't talk about him. Cricket patted her back comforting her. Cricket would be dead, too, if it hadn't been for Raven. He had feed off her when he was turning into a zombie and her blood had cured him. It cured everyone with a heart and the absence of a bullet in their brain.

But it wasn't just last night that Raven saved him. She saved him many years ago when he lived in Africa; Cricket recalls every day. He shared a lot of great times with Jet and the girls. *If my Ray had gone tonight*—Cricket didn't know what he would do if he ever lost Raven. He put his arm around her neck and gently pulled her to him; her head rested just below his chin. It's been so long since he spoke, Cricket wasn't even sure he could form a word let alone a sentence. But if he knew what to say to make everything okay he would try his damnedest.

The cell phone in Cricket's pocket rang and before he even fished it out of his jeans pocket he already knew who it was—Olsen. The two of them had been sending text messages all day; filling each other in on what happened on their sides of the planet. Turns out the disease never left the United States. Raven wasn't much up for talking so it fell to Cricket to tell Olsen that three of their family members wouldn't be returning to Amsterdam—their home. *Ever.*

"I'll talk to him," Raven said and the Shadow handed over the phone.

"Hey," she said into the mouthpiece.

"It's good to finally hear your voice," Cricket heard Olsen say.

"Yeah."

"When are you coming home?"

"It's going to be a long time." Raven said and unexpectedly hung up on Olsen. And Cricket closed his eyes. Cricket knew what Raven said was true so he did the only thing he could do; he held his Raven and rocked her to sleep.

Nebraska

LOKI

Loki perched on the windowsill and stared up at the waning moon shining over the flat prairie grass down below her bedroom window. Her bedroom was two stories up and it faced opposite the direction of Lana's house; her neighbor. Lana's was the only other house around here; the land stretched out for miles and trees were scattered acres apart.

The cool air nipped at her exposed hands and heart-shaped face. But it didn't bother her as much as the new bruise on her right eye. Granted this didn't hurt nearly as much as the cutting her mother used to inflict upon her or the burning of the flesh with the hot end of a cigarette when she was younger. Those incidents stopped when her father, then married to her mom, found out and got her professional help. Years went by and everything was fine. Physically. Her parents got into more and more arguments which oddly resulted in her mom hitting her dad; it was just one of the many factors that contributed to their separation.

After the divorce her dad signed off on all parental rights and moved to another state to be with another woman. If Loki had known that her mother was going to turn into a full blown alcoholic, resulting in the woman taking out all of her problems on her only child, then Loki would have begged to live with her father. But she couldn't have known and when it all started happening Loki didn't want to change schools let alone states. Loki either bailed when the woman finally did decide to show up or she'd fight back. But after personally being turned into a zombie, and then afterwards reverting back to her normal self to find out she lost one of her closest friends, Cole, Loki wasn't much up for fighting or leaving the house so she just took the "punishment". The punishment of being gone and taking the guns without permission.

Now the seventeen year old had two matching black eyes; the one from Raven earlier today was swollen but the one she received from her mother was looking to make a name for itself. Loki lit the cigarette she easily stole from her mom after she passed out on the couch. "Happy Mother's Day," Loki said and blew smoke out her bedroom window. Loki let the thoughts come to her—nasty evil thoughts; thoughts of payback, thoughts of revenge. And not all of them had to do with her abhorrence for Raven... But since she was the thing Loki hated the most, taking Raven down was at the top of the list...

Lana's House

Mrs. Queen (Demon)

"This is going to be so easy," Mrs. Queen—rather the Demon living in her body—whispered into the woman's cellphone, "She hasn't a clue!" Mrs. Queen hung up and went back to her room. She stood over Lana and watched the teenage girl while she slept; her guard completely down. The two of them had talked over dinner; about Kronos setting her on fire and how the Shadow learned to use the Connection; so now the girl could call on other Shadows for help by using her mind. They cleaned the dishes afterwards and as soon as the sun went down the Shadow was off to bed in her mother's room. The Demon even helped tuck the girl's tiny body in under the covers.

Lightning flashed a whitish-blue color on the other side of the flowered pattern curtains and the wind picked up outside; sweeping through the Nebraskan plain and slapping the window with rain. The Demon was positive the Shadow was in a deep sleep. Mrs. Queen reached down and tugged on the lamp string turning it off; the Shadow had wanted it on because it would help her sleep but the Demon didn't care what the little brat wanted. Mrs. Queen smiled as they were left in the dark…

HOME

LANA

Lana rolled over; eyes closed. Her slumber had started out comfortable; as comfortable as possible after teaming up with the cousins and a Vampire Goddess in order to save herself and others from zombies. The sweet melon smell of her mother's pillow and comforter temporarily helped her forget the fact that yesterday she killed one of the few people from high school that gave her the time of day—positive time. Who didn't tease her and make jokes about the scars on her face. She didn't really care what the others said at school. And she cared even less now that high school was over and the Vampire responsible for her physical scars and killing her father is dead. Capital D-E-A-D. Kronos was gone—the permanent kind of gone.

"Lana." A female voice whispered her name. "Lana." The doorknob on her mother's closet turned, and Lana's eyelids fluttered furiously as thunder rumbled softly outside and whitish blue light flashed on the closet door. It creaked open and a dirty hand slipped out; dirty fingers gripped the side of the open door.

"Lana," the voice whispered again, only it was masculine. BOOM! Thunder roared and the door banged open and startled Lana. A bloody Cole— head intact on his shoulders—lunged across the room. Lana tried to fling herself off the bed but her legs became entangled in the sheets. Cole, dirty and bleeding from his face, leaped over the footing and onto the bed with her. When he grabbed her by the shoulders Lana realized her heart was beating

faster than the drops of water falling from the sky and she couldn't move. Cole opened his mouth and whispered, "Save her!"

The picture frame from her mom's nightstand suddenly rose up by itself and hit the side of her forehead. Lana collapsed to the bed...

The aching in her temple caused the Shadow to snap up, fully alert, and she immediately wiped her fingers across the wetness on her forehead. Lightning broke through the darkness of the room and Lana clearly saw blood on her fingers. She reached for the lamp's string dangling from the lamp next to her mom's bed but when she pulled it nothing happened. Rain suddenly pelted against the window and another streak of light from the sky brightened the room just long enough for her to see the picture frame on the floor...

Lana quickly threw the covers off and ran to the light switch. Once again electricity failed the panicking girl. Lana figured the power must be out and went back to the nightstand. She fumbled through the top drawer until she found a flashlight. Lana snapped the light on and searched for the picture frame that was supposed to be on the nightstand but for some reason it was on the floor. Puzzled, Lana bent down and examined the picture of her with her parents before Kronos killed one of them. The glass in the frame was cracked and there was a trace of blood on one of the corners.

This hit me in my dream... how did...? Her thoughts lead back to Cole. And for no logical reason Lana tossed the cracked picture frame onto the bed and ran to the closet and flung open the door…

The faint orange light shined on her mother's clothes; which consisted of business attire, a variety of casual clothes, and a small selection of dresses. Lana shined the light to the left and right of the hanging garments. Nothing but shoes and shoes and more shoes. *What did I expect? Cole? How could he possible come back from having his head severed? A head that I personally took off. But who hit me? In the dream…* Lana thought back. *In the dream it…* Then something occurred to her. She couldn't feel any presence of a Vampire in the house or anywhere close by. *Human…?*

Thunder boomed and Lana whipped around; her heart increased in rhythm and she feared the intruder might be hiding closer than she had thought…under the bed. She slowly crept forward and tried hard to hear signs of movement, signs of someone breathing. She suddenly stopped, not wanting to get too close for someone to grab her ankles. *What is waiting for me underneath there? Someone had to have hit me… I certainly didn't hit myself.*

Lana quickly and bravely dropped down on her knees and hands. She couldn't decide which was worse. What she feared was there; undetected Vampire, human criminal, zombie Cole, Kronos even—or what she saw now? *No. This is much worse.* The thing before her, or rather the empty space of nothing, meant someone attacked her and then left the room. They could very well be hurting or have hurt her mother.

The door to the bedroom suddenly opened

behind her and Lana was swiftly back to her feet ready to attack. "Oh dear!" the startled woman exclaimed holding tightly to a lit candle. "Is something the matter, Lana?" Lana realized she nearly threw the flashlight at her own mom...

LOKI

Loki had previously closed the window to her bedroom when the rain picked up but now it had significantly slowed down. She reopened the window and propped herself on the sill with her back against the frame and her legs on the inside of the house. The wind lightly tossed her blonde curls much to her annoyance. She pulled her hair up into a ponytail using the tie on her wrist. And then Loki watched. She had nothing to do but watch the rain and think.

"You're a bad parent, mother. You will get what's coming to you. And so will Raven," Loki whispered maliciously into the night. The spring rain virtually came to a halt, and something moved down below; her gray eyes grew when she spotted a Cottontail Rabbit poking around in the grass. Loki leaned back inside the window and reached for the BB gun half hidden by her curtains. She intensely watched the rabbit as it hoped closer to the house. It had most likely come out from its underground shelter due to flooding caused by the downpour. Loki didn't like the idea that it thought it could escape death by sneaking across her yard. She pulled the trigger and the furry long-eared creature squealed. Loki was sure she only hit it in the ear and she prepared to fire again. But the rabbit quickly hopped away using the darkness as a shield. Loki didn't kill it, but she still smiled with wicked satisfaction.

"This entire world will get what it deserves," the teenager stated and swung her legs back inside the unlit room and dropped the BB gun on her carpeted floor. She closed the window shut and stripped down to her undergarments, and then pulled back her bedspread. "It's just a matter of time," Loki smiled and closed her bruised eyes; her ambition was just beginning…

~~~

Chapter 2
Flash me Back

October
Present Day

I SIT DOWN ON MY bed and open my cousin's journal. I'm curious as to what Leon writes about; until recently I didn't even know he did this weird journaling thing.

May 12

I awoke to the wonderful aroma of bacon being fried. I knew what this meant. I tossed the covers off and stretched before hopping out of my old bed. I was wearing the flannel pajama bottoms I left at Uncle's, and I practically jogged passed Lucas sleeping on his stomach and drooling on his pillow. It was just like old times—us sharing a room and waking up to a warm delicious breakfast—which is what I wanted very much when I burst into my uncle's kitchen just like the kid I was years ago. Except zombies didn't exist then. But at least they are extinct now and my family survived!

"Sup, sleepyhead?" Rachel said from the kitchen table when I walked in. Her country accent is so funny. It's worse than Luke's. But I have noticed that our accents get thicker the longer we are home. I kissed Rachel on the cheek and playfully tugged on her long black hair that she had tied in a high ponytail. "Zombies might not have gotten those pretty blues but those eye boogers sure did."

I laughed and wiped the corners of my eyes. "Out of your pajamas already?"

"Someone had to feed the animals."

I looked at the clock on the microwave:

11:30. We usually take turns tending to the cows, chickens, goats, and pigs and whatever needs to be fixed on Uncle's small farm, but I just couldn't do it this time. My little sister (basically since we are so close) she didn't mind, but still, I felt a pang of guilt. She had probably just finished. I know she has to be tired of getting up early and just tired of doing it in general. Both of us worry about what happens when Rachel leaves for college in August…? Everyone's most likely to be gone, doing something, so no one will be here to take care of him—I mean help him.

(I knew Leon meant the other. We both worried about my uncle's well-being and the lack of a woman in his life.)

Either way he can't do it by himself; for one, that back of his just isn't getting better and he refuses to take any more money from me…

"What time did you guys stroll in?" Rachel asked me after taking a giant gulp of OJ.

"Last night."

"The morning night," my uncle said standing over the griddle. He picked up the cooked strips of bacon and placed them on a plate that was covered in paper towels to soak up the grease.

Lucas and I arrived when it was still dark outside and we decided to crash at Uncle Joe's place. Why wouldn't we? It's the house I grew up in after a Vampire killed my—

(He must have really felt something here 'cause he just stopped. I don't get why Leon can't really talk about it after all these years.)

Lucas and I have been searching for Avy, but have yet to find so much as a clue. It seems odd not a single Vampire has heard of him or knows anything... Not even Raven... But I guess she can't know everyone or everything in the world.

I sat down and joined Rachel. "Eben here?"

"Left an hour ago," answered my Uncle while he cracked my eggs over the griddle.

"Did he say where?"

"Does he ever?" Rachel retorted and bit into a strip of bacon. (It's rare that I ask about my brother's whereabouts, but with zombies taking over the states I was actually concerned. Although he could probably care less if I dropped dead right now.) The three of us talked some more, and not long after I got up Lucas walked into the kitchen. His blonde hair was groomed and he was dressed in his shop clothes. I knew something was up.

"Morning, skank," Rach addressed him.

"Morning." Luke said in the most unexpected way.

"That's it?" she asked disappointedly. Name calling was their way of bonding and communicating. "Man, what all happened west of the Mississippi River?"

Lucas passed by us and took his car keys off the hook by the refrigerator. "Gotta get to work," is what he said. Work? Really??? I couldn't believe him!

"The shop is fine, son. Sit down and—"
"See you later," Luke nonchalantly cut Joe off as he headed out the front door.

The two of them stared at me waiting for me to explain Lucas's ditching behavior. "Is there something you haven't told us?" asked Uncle Joe. I sighed and just told them (him and Rachel) the truth; no omitting—something I'm sure Luke is going to love…

B.L.C

HOME

I close my cousin's journal and my stomach turns. The love of my life was buried yesterday. Why did I think that reading from a journal was going to cure me? Because it definitely didn't and now I feel like I'm going to be sick. I flash back to that day…the one he talked about; a cute girl came into the shop to pick her car up and I flirted with her at the front desk. The phone rang and one of my mechanics answered it. "Hey, someone named Raven is on the phone for you."

"Tell her I'm at lunch," I told Brad to lie. Later I saw my uncle when he pulled up in his Dodge. I had a bad feeling about this and I told Brad to lie to him also by saying I was at lunch. "You're just dodging everyone today, huh?" I shrugged his question off and disappeared to my office in the back. I sat behind my desk and just stared at the computer screen waiting for my uncle to leave. "Leon told me what happened," my uncle suddenly barged in like a scary knight ready to slaughter something. I didn't expect the back door to come flinging wide open and I nearly tumbled over in my chair. "That was supposed to be locked," I mumbled sourly.

"We can do this now or later. But you got to talk sometime. I know where you work and where you live, son," Uncle Joe pointed out, and leaned back against the filing cabinet. His gray hair, that had recently started coming in, seemed to make him more intimating. But I would never tell him that.

"What did he tell you?"

"Raven called Leon not long ago," he cut to the chase. "Cole's service is in Hastings on the thirteenth, and Jet, Sheba, and Ganesha's is on the fourteenth. Or the fifteenth in Amsterdam. The time zone has me all confused. Leon has the details. So why's he called Cricket?" Joe asked off handedly, and added right just as he turned to leave, "Anyhow, I thought you should attend one of those."

"Why?"

"For support. *Duh!*"

"People die every day. What makes her so special?" I immediately steered the conversation towards Raven.

"She died for us. For *you*," he said and turned back for the door, but I stopped him. "I told her things. We were on a rooftop and the world was going to hell and I told her things. Things that left the impression that I might…" *Like her.*

The most intimidating man I have ever known flat-out asked me, "What are you afraid of Lucas? That she doesn't like you? Or that you like her?" Uncle Joe got right down it, preventing me from further lying to him and myself. I looked up at my uncle and instantly I knew that my eyes had betrayed me, admitting the latter. "I guess Leon just has to tell you everything."

"He didn't tell me anything about your lovey-dovey feelings," uncle clarified. "You know, when you were growing up the house may have looked like a billy goat lived in there with us, but you sure as hell weren't raised by one. I'm not an idiot, son. And let me tell you this; from what I know of luck, I am betting that one of those Vampires and whatcha-ma-call-its—Shadows—didn't die in

Nebraska."

Realization spread across my face.

"That's right. Someone or something is coming for all of ya. Leon's plan involves going to a funeral. I suggest you figure out yours. Fast."

The sun was still up in the air, much like my mind when I left the shop. The ride through town went by in a blur, for there was only one thing on my mind.

Uncle Joe.

Before I knew it I had taken the back way home; not my usual route. I was at the only unpaved four-way in our city and I turned left unto my dirt road. The road is extremely long and there are only three houses on it; mine, Uncle Joe's, and our neighbor Wally. My house is the center one no matter which direction I came from. My Uncle Joe lives about a mile away from me, and my neighbor lives about two miles from me. After I passed by Wally's, I turned right unto my long, graveled driveway. I immediately recognized the large truck parked out front—Leon's.

The two of us built this house ourselves from the ground up; two bedrooms, each with their own bathroom, and a guest bedroom that included a full bath. The guest bedroom is the front of the house and it faces out to nothing but grass and the field across the street.

I'm was halfway up the driveway when I realized I must have made up my mind. I had left some stuff at my uncle's and I wasn't planning on going back for it anytime soon. I planned on avoiding Uncle Joe for as long as possible. I had no intentions of leaving the state—unless, of course, some poor soul needed saving from Vampires. I parked beside Leon and just then I wished my *truth-telling* cousin would get a vision. I desperately wanted to get away from all of this.

Slowly I walked to the side of the house, up the steps, across the porch, and I let the screen door slam behind me as I entered the living room; ready for my cousin's lecture of the day. But I wasn't expecting Uncle Joe to be sitting at the kitchen table, which I had a direct view of as I entered the house. *Great.* I stopped in my tracks and decided quickly to get to the point. "Are you really flying over there?" I asked Leon.

"Why not?" he shrugged.

"So, Brighton," I gritted his first name through my teeth as I entered the kitchen. "You really just gonna get over your fear of flyin'?"

"Yeah. Pretty much, Lucas," he said in a way that sounded a lot like condemnation and that I should just get over my fear as well. "Yeah, well…I'm NOT," I fought back, and took a beer out of the refrigerator. "And I am *not* going to Amsterdam. Or any other place that requires I take a chance on falling out of the sky." I popped the top off and put the beer to my lips.

"Tell me you're not going to hide behind that excuse," Leon called me out.

"I am not *hiding*. I am right here. In Tennessee. I will be right here if Raven or anyone else needs help with killing Vampires." Or Demons. I just wasn't sure yet on how exactly I was supposed to get rid of a *Demon* from *Hell*. But that wasn't the issue. I started for the living room again, and I heard a chair suddenly turn over and bounce off the ground. I turned back around and witnessed my uncle marching out of the house.

A knot began to form in my throat. My uncle was beyond mad. I couldn't recall the last time Uncle Joe marched out of a conversation. I didn't like what happened between us, and apparently my decision to stay on the ground and not up in the sky also upset Leon. We only exchanged a few words after uncle left but it was enough to send him over to Joe and Rachel's; so I sat in front of the TV drinking beer by myself.

I wasn't too much affected by my cousin's issue with my decision. I figured there was no way that he was really getting on an airplane. After our first and only plane ride we were terrified and vowed never to air travel. I pictured my cousin showing up to the airport trying to be all heroic and then totally running away with his tail in between his legs. There wasn't much we were afraid of, but to me the fear of flying was second place behind our previous encounter with the walking dead. Zombies and flying would always be my two bug-a-boo's.

But the way my uncle left…my conscience was getting to me. "Crap," I said aloud to myself, irritated, while I finished off my fourth beer. I sat, more like slammed, the empty glass bottle on the coffee table and headed to the back of the house. I decided it was a great time to get my stuff. Once outside I began the mile long jog through the woods to my uncle's place.

I didn't know what I was going to say; to either

one of them really. I remember thinking *The time difference. Amsterdam… Raven's is hours ahead. If I was going I would have to leave tomorrow…* Maybe I planned on explaining that flying just wasn't an option. I wasn't even sure why Leon even cared that I stayed here. Without me around it would have been the perfect time for him to make a move on Raven.

I saw Rachel sitting outside as I busted into the clearing towards the front of the wraparound porch. She was playing on her phone; texting I assumed. "I'm guessing you said no," she said to me looking up from her phone.

"You know why I can't go."

"I haven't seen dad this upset since Eben set those fires." Eben's juvenile act had permanently made him the black sheep of the family. I was never going to forgive him for what he did. "If you aren't gonna say *yes* then I wouldn't go in there."

"I left some stuff here."

I heard a car strolling up the driveway; familiar with the engines struggling sound. "Dude, I hope it's worth dying over. Obviously whatever you said pissed him off." The car's headlights beamed in my face and Rachel's friend, Emily, dimmed the lights. "I am so staying out of this," Rach said, and hopped in the backseat of the car because someone else was in the front.

Emily u-turned in the gravel part of the yard and I saw another set of lights coming up to the house. I knew who it was; it wasn't the position of the headlights that gave him away but the noise punching your eardrums in the form of bad heavy metal that easily rocked the air and vibrated windows. I didn't have much time to think about Eben. Uncle Joe flew outside and tossed me my stuff. And on top of things, Leon shoved a ticket in my hand. "What is this? You two ganging up on me like usual?" I saw Uncle Joe's jaw tighten, and Leon replied, "It's not like that."

I was about to say something but Joe came down the stairs, and his face became uncomfortably close to mine. "If you don't go, don't you *ever* set foot in my house again."

Eben walked by and decided to put his two cents in. "About time. I could go without seeing your ugly face."

"Are you kidding me?" I asked my uncle distastefully. "After all the shitty things he has done *he* gets to stay *here*? But *I* have to leave?"

"Go home, Lucas," my uncle told me. And I realized I didn't have many options. Just before Eben opened the front door he flashed me a look so smug and cocky I had to lash out. "I'm always going to be a better brother for Leon than you." "So," Eben shrugged before going inside the house.

Now I feel like I must write.

October 6

It's morning right now...

I don't know if it was my cousin Eben's attitude, or admitting the fact that my Uncle was right... But when May 13 came rushing upon me I was on that flight to Amsterdam.

I didn't leave with Joe when he came to pick us up that morning though. And I fought with myself before calling on Rachel to drop me off at the airport. I barely made it on the plane in time. Leon said something to me but I told him not to talk to me. He didn't listen. "Look I know flying—

"I love you, but if you don't stop talking..." I threatened and he dropped it and looked out the tiny window. Out of all of the times to fly I pick the 13 hour flight! I threw up twice and nearly got a bladder infection from holding my urine! I finally realized that maybe it really was okay to move around. After relieving myself I was finally able to sleep.

I don't even know why I was angry but I was. I was on an airplane. It was scary and terrifying and I sure as hell didn't like it. I <u>hated</u> it. And what's worse is that the idea of seeing Raven was much worse. Also, when Leon woke me up to tell me we were

landing I really disliked his stupid calm face. But I am glad he was there.

I stop writing and pick up Lana's Diary. I know what I was doing on the thirteenth, but what was Lana doing? It feels kind of intrusive coming to know a Shadow—Lana—like this... But they did tell me it was okay...

May 14

It was just the three of us yesterday; Cole's parents (adopted) and me. The ceremony was already ten minutes behind schedule and I knew we must start soon. "May I use your phone?" I asked Cole's mom.

"Certainly. I still don't understand why you girls don't have cell phones. And why Cole had one and never used it."

"Loki's mom still won't let her have one. And I didn't really need one since I only have two friends—" Had. I went inside his parents' house and called Loki. Nothing but the ringing noise. I had called Loki yesterday and told her Cole's memorial service was today. Loki said that she would show. But so far the only thing there right then was a sinking suspicion in

my gut.

I hung up the phone and returned back to the memorial site in the backyard—a place at the back of the house right smack in the middle of the flower beds. Cole's mother held the cross in her trembling hands; the one Cole's father carved. His dad dug a small hole with a shovel and then gently took the wooden cross from his wife's hands and planted it in the earth. And then Jessica wiped away the tears on her face with a tissue. She began by saying how blessed she was to have Cole for a son.

And then my own feelings muffled the rest of her words. The man and the woman I know so well were trying to deal with the fact that their only child isn't coming back, and my tears silently purged that I killed him. Not directly of course. It was a Vampire's fault that Cole got infected. But if I had played into the idea there was a cure then he would still be alive.

I didn't like being there by myself; his parents' presence just wasn't the same. It was hard trying to say goodbye to one friend while worrying about the other. I tried not to worry too much. The three of

us embraced each other and for a moment everything was okay. But then it was my turn to speak and the small huddle broke, reminding me that it isn't okay. I sniffled to keep from further crying.
To be continued.
L. Queen

I feel bad. About what I'm not sure. Lana's a sweet girl. I stare at my journal and my mind jumps back to Amsterdam. The service, Raven, and Olsen Courtney. I breathe and try to control my anger.

October 6 (Continued)

Our plane landed in Amsterdam at 2am on May 14 (it was 7pm back home and just now getting dark). Cricket was waiting for us at the airport with a limousine that took us to Raven's...mansion. That was just one of many things that I was so overwhelmed by. I was just glad I'd worn the right clothes. It was chilly there.

That night (morning night as Joe would call it) Leon and I slept in the world's most comfortable beds. I will never forget that night. I was out of place. Yet I felt like I belonged there. I thought about Raven and if she was sleeping. Strangely, it has been one of the better nights of sleep.

But then Leon woke up with a strange text from Cricket. That he, Raven, and Olsen, would meet us at the service. That someone would arrive at noon to take us there. Just after we arrived inside Cricket sent Leon another text saying they couldn't find Ray anywhere and it was past time to start the service. I didn't have much time to panic because I nearly got punched.

"Lucas I presume?" His annoying voice approached me from behind. I of course didn't know who he was so 'WHO THE HELL?' Is what went through my mind as I turned around. Mr. Wanna-be-Oliver Queen from Smallville was standing there. The same lame blonde-pretty-boy hairstyle and everything. "Yeah," I said. "What's it to you?"

"What's it to me??" He rhetorically asked before coming at me full speed, intending to punch my face. Cricket intercepted, keeping me from taking a blow to my jaw. "What did you do to her?" Pretty Boy damn near yelled in front of everyone there.

I rubbed my jaw, thinking. I was mad at what he was about to do. And mad about what was currently happening. But when I looked into Olsen's eyes I knew. I knew in that moment that this was the worst that he had ever been scared. And that he thought I was somehow responsible for that. Which made me very happy.

"You did something to Raven I know it," he continued. "Or else she would be here."

"Maybe you did something. Do that again and I'll do something."

"I'm okay." Her voice stopped whatever was happening between me and him— temporarily. I will never forget the first time I met Olsen Courtney. What a clown. A bad one. Not that there's a good one really. I'm rambling.

Back to her voice. Raven's. I believe it was the first time I had heard it in 2 days. I'm certain that if someone had asked me what the greatest noise in the world was I would have lied and said the sound of a female before climax. It's a nice sound, usually, but nothing and no one could make me feel the way Raven did. I'm not a love sick puppy. It's just a fact. I can't label what we are, what-who she was to me. She was...great.

"Olsen, I'm here," she slipped her hand onto Pretty Boy's shoulder. Whatever feelings of happiness I might have had

quickly dispersed when he responded with, "I love you," and put his arms around her waist. Everything suddenly flared up inside of me. Not just jealousy—I now know. Just... Everything.

The phone in my pants buzzed. It was Cricket texting me: They have history. INTENSE history. Now calm down.

I expected that about as much as I expected to be there. Strangely I composed myself like a real adult. Olsen started the service and I sat on the bench next to Leon. Raven was in between him and Cricket. I kept expecting her to cry but she never did. I tried my best not to look at her. I didn't know what to do. How to comfort her...? What I would say afterwards...? What happens afterwards period?

There was a moment between me and Raven at the service. I didn't know it then. I should have and all of this could have been avoided... I should have made Raven mine. But I didn't.

No amount of writing will change that.
—Lucas Kale

HOME

I suddenly wonder what kinds of things Ray put in her diary. She kept one. I just don't know where. But I know where to start looking.

Immediately I get up and begin the hunt while in my boxers. Just as I open my bedroom door I remember that Leon took the day off, and I see that he slept with his door wide-open. *Lovely. I'm pretty sure that if he sees me he's going to think I'm acting suspicious!* Not wanting him to catch me in the act, or catch me at all, I nonchalantly tip-toe past his room directly on the left side of mine (if I were in it) and beeline it to Raven's room. *Am I bad at this kind of thing, or is it his annoying genius brain?*

I haven't wasted a second and I quickly and very lightly shut Ray's door behind me. I gasp and almost freak out for a second. Her scent is so strong it's almost like she never left. She's been gone about a week so I know different. I know all too well.

I try real hard to think like her. *Where would I put my diary? Not the obvious places; beside the bed, the panty drawer, not even the closet. Where would someone like me not look?* I saw the row of Bibles and references on her bookshelf. I scanned the items. There it was. It blended in but she wasn't fooling me. I snatch it out from in-between a thick bible and an even thicker reference book. I open to the first page just to make sure I haven't gone crazy. Looks like a diary. I really want to read it, but now isn't the time. Leon does like sleeping in but he usually doesn't sleep in for long. Realizing I have nowhere to hide this thing if I get caught sends me into a weird panic. I don't know why it matters if he catches me, it's not like Raven's going to mind me reading it. I quickly and silently bolt out of her room, past my cousin's bedroom, and back to my own.

Feeling like I got away with something, I eagerly flop down on my bed and breathe. Relieved. I shake away the adrenaline that came with my thievery and I lay back against the headboard. *I can't believe I have her diary!* It does feel kind of wrong, but at the same time this is like my ticket aboard *The Polar Express*.

HOME

May

Cricket laid his head on my shoulder and wept. Olsen was speaking but I'm not sure I heard even a word. I can't claim I'm lost, moving about as if in a daze—time is different though, but I would say that's from being all human now. No, I wasn't lost. I knew exactly where I was. On a bench. Back in Amsterdam. I know heartfelt words were spoken about our Jet and Ganesha. I know Sheba's father took the floor in her behalf. His wife had died that very morning from breast cancer, and in some ways I felt the old man was the closest person to me. What he had wasn't much but he loved them and he lost all he had.

Olsen has lost a lot...but there will always be a distance between us. Before, when I was...half... Vampire. The word seems strange. Everything is strange. Seeing, smelling, hearing, emotions even. Back to what I was saying. When I was part Vampire I had forgave Olsen for what he had done. But I knew I could never be in love with him. To this day I still feel like that's true.

I heard Olsen's words but I didn't know what they meant. Jet was dead. Ganesha was dead. And Sheba was (presumed) dead. All these years I have been unable to die and now I can finally do so. The fact that I could die should make me happy. But they are dead and that's my fault. I didn't take my so called place with the Vampires.

Being able to die is something I have always wanted, but I feel like it came at a price. And well, I guess it did. I want to be angry at God, but what would be the point? I didn't know. What was the point in all of this? The trees? Plants? I don't know anything. What to feel? What to think? What to do next?

I guess I might have zoned out because Olsen wasn't talking anymore and people started chattering amongst themselves. Some started removing the decorations. I don't know how they got there in the first place. I had no part in their orchestration. Some people came up to me and gave their condolences in some way and in return I would reply "Thank you". They are but a blur to me now.

I made eye contact with Lucas and he did something I didn't expect. He was suddenly looking down at me and he cupped my face in his hands and kissed my forehead.

"Raven," Olsen gently said and I let him lead me away from Lucas. I don't know why, I guess because Olsen has been good to me and he means a lot to me as well.

He put his arm around me and said, "Let's go home." <u>Home</u>? I thought. He means to the empty house. How can that ever be home again??

I just want to forget. Forget them. Forget me. That part should be easy considering I don't even know who I am. I'm not a god. I'm not an all-powerful being. I'm not strong and my tissues don't regenerate. I have lived forever and now I will die. It's what I've always wanted. To be human.

But what the hell is that???

I don't know what happened next exactly... I felt weird, but I knew it would be alright—Lucas Kale was there. Everything went black…

I pick up my pen again.

October 6 (Continued)

Raven fainted and I caught her from behind. You want me to admit I was worried? Well, yeah I was. But I discovered she was breathing so that was a huge f-ing relief. I was worried as was Leon and Cricket and that Buttface Blondie. I failed to realize this at the time, but Ray knew it and she played us. <u>She</u> suggested going to the hospital to be checked out instead of going to their mansion. I think we wanted to do that anyways because she was now human. I would have taken her to the hospital regardless.

Just wish I could have been the first to realize she was just on the run. At least before Olsen did.

—Lucas Kale

* * *

(Past/May)

LOKI
&
MRS.QUEEN

Loki looked down at her phone. LANA'S MOM. "Hello, dear," the voice was that of sweet Mrs. Queen. "I'm on my way," Loki told her.

With her and Lana being neighbors and all, it didn't take long for Loki to jog up the only hill in Nebraska and run across her friend's giant field. The run wasn't bad. She could see how someone a little overweight might not think so. But she had been running in these fields since birth. She excitedly ran up the stairs to the black colored deck. Loki was a little apprehensive about running into Lana with her newest punishment displayed on her heart-shaped face but she couldn't wait to hear the news!

Lana's mom was waiting right inside the basement for her. Only it wasn't Lana's mother and Loki knew it; long before the woman's eyes changed color revealing her true self. "By the look on your face I'm assuming you're going to have plenty of fun."

Loki's gray eyes were bright and wide with a mischievous kind of lust, similar to that found in a small child. "Oh, there will be lots of fun." She accepted the piece of paper from Mrs. Queen's hands. "What do you remember?" the Demon asked her.

"Everything. Her blood not only brought me

back but it showed me who she is. Who I AM." Loki unfolded the paper and read the Tennessean address. "Let the good times roll." Loki turned and as the screen door closed behind her on the way out she heard the Demon say, "Keep the boys occupied for Avy and me."

Loki smiled. "Oh you can count on that. If there's one thing I've learned since the zombie outbreak is that I shouldn't wait on my mother to come to her senses. And I'm having some fun this summer." This was the most excited the seventeen year old had ever been in her entire life. Nothing or anyone was going to prevent her from carrying through with her plan. Loki knew who she was now. Who Raven was—her undeniable nemesis.

And Loki looked forward to war…

~~~~

Chapter 3
Again, Please

October 7
Present Day

I'M DEFINITELY HUNG-OVER. I have no idea what I did last night... Raven fainting comes to mind. I now recall writing about it but nothing afterwards. There is no way I can bring myself to see what's after Raven's previous entry. Ray left off with her fainting at the service.

But I do know what I'm about to see. I untangle my legs from my sheet's death grip, and I leap out of bed and run to my bathroom. I taste cheap beer, but it's nachos I see in the toilet. *When did I have nachos?* Wait...cheap beer and nachos can only mean one thing. Xbox with Leon. Drunken Xbox-shooting-and-killing-with Leon. Wait... I remember making these nachos. I remember Leon laughing hysterically as we dumped sour cream on them. I can't remember why this was funny. *Wasted. That's why.* I brush my teeth and then leave the bathroom. Walking like a zombie, I stumble out of my bedroom and into the small dining/kitchen area to my right.

"Guess I'm not going to work," I mumble as I enter the kitchen, realizing it's dark out when I glance out the backdoor. The microwave beeps and Leon pulls out some popcorn, and I see that he has cleaned whatever mess we made the night before. I open the frig and drink the last of the OJ, straight from the jug. "Hey Sleeping Beauty," Leon greets me with a lopsided grin and takes his bag of popcorn to the living room.

It's an open kitchen, no door and it has an opening that's meant to be like a bar so I have a clear view of the living room. Last night had been fun. And that's good because now I feel sick—I realize why my cousin was making popcorn. According to the commercial, HALLOWEENTOWN is playing tonight. It's one of Leon's favorite Halloween flicks and I should have known he wasn't going to miss it. Especially with how much Ray loved Halloween. I'm pretty sure he will get involved with anything Halloween related now. Honoring her memory.

He sure is a lot better at this me, I silently admit to myself. I want to have the Halloween spirit. I want a lot of things. But right now the only spirit I have is this bag of bricks attached to this anchor buried inside of me.

I hadn't paid any attention, but now I'm surveying the kitchen and living room. I don't know where the decorations in here keep coming from, Leon obviously, but more and more seem to be popping up in the house day by day. It's not going to take long for Leon to have this place immersed inside and out with skeletons, ghosts, and all things 'vampires'. He used to say that was truly the scariest part of Halloween because they're real. But now I think it's a tie between Vampires and Ghosts.

I kill the last of the orange juice with two ibuprofen and flee back to my *Halloween-free* dungeon, and away from the fluorescents that's not helping my headache. I'm positive that when Leon finishes with our place he's going to carry on with his decoration spree at Uncle Joe's. *Ugh!*

Back in my room, I feel like my skin is melting and I take my shirt off and toss it to the floor somewhere and then throw myself onto the bed. I land on Lana's dairy. I guess I forgot to hide it under my bed along with Raven's and the other two journals. I happily resume reading.

May 14 (continued)

"You're always welcome over, Lana." Cole's mom told me when she dropped me off. And there was Loki unexpectedly walking down the steps of my deck. She now had 2 black eyes. We talked about her new black eye and her taking off to the south. Loki told me she had to make an emergency visit to Tennessee because her mom is possessed by a Demon... That's why she has another black eye.

I asked her why she couldn't stay with me and my mom and why she couldn't just call... And then she asked me things I hadn't thought about... "How long can you protect your mom, Lana? She already knows everything. Don't you wonder if she ever thinks about the noises she hears when getting in her car at night? Is it a Vampire? A creeper? Or a zombie making a comeback? Do you really want her going to sleep at night knowing she is neighbors with a Demon? And there is nothing she can do about it? What happens when the Demon knows that she knows?"

These were all very good questions. Loki also pointed out that she (herself) may be putting us in danger by her staying at my house. I knew my mom wasn't going to move out without me telling her why. The <u>real</u> why.

"It's okay. I'm moving into the dorms soon anyway. WE are. I'm going to Tennessee with or without you." She informed me.

And then I came up with a lie on why I had to leave. I didn't feel right about leaving her so soon, but my mom not only told me to go to Tennessee but she also gave me her cell phone!

So Loki and I left for TN that night on the 13. We arrived at Joe's house in the morning. Raven, Lucas, Leon, and Cricket arrived around 7 pm. But during this time Loki painted Raven in a bad light to Rachel. Talking about how rich Raven is and how she was playing Lucas and Leon. I told her to tone it down and she said she would, but I'm pretty sure Loki said or did

something behind my back. I don't know what has gotten into my friend...she's... I tried to smooth things over with Rachel but the damage has already been done. Rachel said she was fine but clearly she isn't as thrilled about meeting Raven...
              L. Queen

That was true. I don't really want to think about when we got back from Amsterdam. Everything was intense to say the least. And now it suddenly occurs to me I have Cricket's journal. He doesn't speak so I am extremely curious as what he had to say. Before, I did wonder what was in here but... I guess I wasn't ready to listen to a man of no words. Cricket's journal feels different from the rest. His is soft and made out of some expensive material. With care, I open to the first page. The only thing written is *Cricket's Chronicles* in dark green ink in the middle of the page. I scan ahead. There doesn't appear to be near as many entries as the others. I go back to the beginning. It isn't dated.

HOME

Lucas got a phone call—Loki was at Uncle Joe's. The Hunters' uncle. Loki said there was a Demon in her mother.

(I gather this is when we were in Amsterdam for Sheba, Ganesha's, and Jet's services.)

She was loud enough to hear over Lucas's phone; even without my super hearing. "I didn't think the chances of anyone helping me were good so I came in person," the annoying little girl said. Ray was alarmed about Loki's presence there and said we must hurry back. Olsen didn't want Ray to go. He thought she needed a moment to breathe. And I didn't disagree. Ganesha, Jet, and Sheba are dead, and Ray just fainted after the service. I didn't think this was a battle I needed to partake in.

Olsen ultimately stayed in Amsterdam but we used his private jet to get back to the United States of America. On the way here one of Olsen's doctors took Ray's blood, urine, and some other stuff. And I explained some of the intense history between Ray and Olsen to the Vampire Hunters; that she and Olsen are from the same time period. Him being in another dimension and that he ages slower because of it. And how it was because of Ray's mom that he got trapped there.

I left out the fact, however, that Olsen was there because of the choice he made... I couldn't see any reason for telling anyone this. It's Raven's & Olsen's business. They have both treated me well. No betrayal from me. Betrayal. This brings me to Loki...

Something is off. I don't like Loki. Don't trust her. I'm scared for Lana. I'm scared for all of us. I will pray.

I write this for Raven & Lana. May they always know how much I love them. And for my former friends, Jet, Sheba, and Ganesha—may they rest well. For I fear there is a far off, yet beautiful pit-stop for the rest of us... The journeys will likely be long and different to and from this said place. But here our journeys must cross. And then where shall I lie?

I finish reading—I'm not sure what. *Cricket and his enigmatic self.* I haven't a clue what he is talking about… But it's probably important. I read it again and then my mind jumps to one person. *What did Olsen do to end up in another dimension…?* I plan on interrogating him someday, but not right now. Cricket left me with more questions than answers, and after drinking all night last night there's nothing left in me. Leon taps on my door and announces, "Pizza's here!" *He ordered pizza!* I enthusiastically roll off my stomach, leaving Cricket's journal there on my bed.

HALLOWEENTOWN is of course playing as I trudge out of my dungeon for greasy deliciousness. No matter how well he seems to be handling Raven's death I decide to not make fun of him for watching it; no reason why I should drag him down into my pit of whatever this is. From the kitchen I hear the youngest kid in the movie say, *"Somebody's coming."* I throw two slices of pizza onto the plate that Leon was kind enough to leave out. "Do you want to join me?" he asks from his spot in the living room; right smack in the middle of the couch. "No thanks," I say in between chewing, and bee-line it back to my room. It's been a week since Raven passed away. But I don't want to think about that, or anything Halloween related. *Because this has turned out to be the worst month of my life,* I admit, thinking to myself.

I shut the door behind me and shove the last of that first slice down my throat. *My cousin's a good person.* "Clearly better for Ray than me," I mumble.

I immediately knew it that night we got back from being overseas.

Sleeping arrangements were discussed. Loki and Lana were taking over the old room that Leon and I once shared at our uncle's. Raven suggested she go to a hotel and Rachel agreed in a negative almost hostile way. But much to her and Loki's dismay, Raven ended up staying at our house. Cricket and Lana patrolled looking for vamps to kill and to get information—any kind. Cricket gave Leon a piece of paper as they were leaving my uncle's to go patrolling. It said **Raven can't sleep alone.** But Leon didn't look at it until after we got back to our house so we couldn't ask what that meant. Lana and Cricket were out hunting and we didn't exactly think they would have their cell phones on. But after we showed Ray to the guestroom the both of us agreed to keep an eye on her.

That was the first night Leon and I tried letting Raven sleep by herself. It was bad. Mozart came running in the living room to warn us. But it was too late. Raven started screaming. By the time we got to her she had already scratched herself in places, to the point of bleeding. Her skin and the bed sheets were soaked with her sweat. Apparently Ray had terrible night terrors that started years ago. Like centuries. Now that she was human it was *extremely* awful. The things Ray dreamt about... That time it was zombies—the ones biting her. Eating her alive. I still can't imagine what she went through. Just seeing it was horrible: her flesh, her wrists, shoulders, stomach, and her legs. When they stopped feeding off her Ray was bloodstained and she had a protruding bone; it was sticking out through what little skin she had on her body. It was like overgrown, demented vultures had ripped apart a baby. I shiver and shake my head; jarring away that terrifying moment and jumping back to that night when we discovered Raven suffered from night terrors.

The ex-goddess ended up sleeping with Leon in his bed. Leon gave her a glass of water and told Raven she was safe with him. Due to my cousin habitually sleeping with his door open, I saw them while they slept. They were facing each other peacefully. Even though I wished that was me lying there, I wasn't full blown jealous. I couldn't bring myself to lay beside Raven, to comfort her—no matter how worried I was about her.

Things changed dramatically that morning. Mainly because Raven saw a ghost.

I remember Leon telling me how he originally thought she was freaking out because they were in bed together. But in actuality she was seeing the present; and not the present moment that the two of them shared. *The present moment somewhere else that involved a ghost.*

"A lot of good that gift did her," I say disappointedly to no one other than myself, and devour my second slice of pizza that has just about everything on it; cheese and lots of meat. When I finish I decide that I would rather suffer through Leon's tortuous film about a witch Marnie and her magical adventure than suffer one more second alone in this hellhole. I very hungrily join my nappy-haired cousin in the living room for more than just pizza. I sit down in my recliner; located close to the front door but facing him and the couch. Leon's blue eyes, which mystifies the ladies, gloss over, delighted, and I can practically see all of his teeth he's smiling so big. Leon is clearly stoked that I'm hanging out with him but he doesn't make a big deal out of it. He got barbeque wings. That's something *I'm* stoked about and I sloppily dig in; sauce covering my fingertips and mouth.

Soon it comes to a part in the movie where the kids excitedly put on their costumes given to them by their grandmother. *I wonder what it would be like to have kids... With Raven...*

And then I remember Raven is dead. I head to the kitchen for the beer that's calling my name.

Chapter 4
The Beginning of the Sword

(The Past)

May 15
Tennessee

RAVEN WAS SLIGHTLY FREAKED out when she woke up next to Leon Carmany that morning. At first she was reminded of her current situation—that Demons walk the earth and that one moved inside Loki's mother; that Sheba was once a Shadow, then a zombie, and now she was dead. Then suddenly the view in Leon's room changed. Lights that Leon didn't even have wildly flickered on and off and a woman with short gray hair, dressed in a nightgown, sat crying at the edge of her bed that was sort of in the room with Leon and her… Only Leon wasn't seeing it…

Raven knew what she was witnessing; a poltergeist terrorizing a little old lady. But she couldn't believe it! The experience was like two sceneries merging into one.

Unexpectedly, the hairbrush next to the woman's bed violently flew off the nightstand and across the room. Raven screamed as the brush came at her. That woke Leon up within a quickness. And Leon panicking startled Raven from the old lady and suddenly it was as if Raven were flying backwards, and then she was outside seeing the front of the woman's house. Raven looked around; she saw the street sign and then Leon next to her in his room. He said something to her and the view closed. Whatever was causing her to see the Ghost stopped—the room was back to normal and Raven only saw Leon about to go into hysterics, and Lucas running in with a wooden baseball bat. He had filed its handle into a stake some time ago; before she knew him.

Leon looked up the address after Raven told them everything she had seen and his research told him the street and mailbox number were only in Adams. And then she and Mozart were off to a hunt a Ghost with Brighton Leon Carmany and Lucas Kale.

After traveling several miles in the backseat of the dark blue Biscayne, "through the country" as Leon called it, to a place that seemed to be located in what Lucas referred to as "the sticks", Raven found herself sitting in a tiny house that belonged to a mean and delusional old lady. By the way the old woman had carried on about her dead grandson's ungratefulness, it was obvious he was the dead guy haunting the house.

And Raven's patience was becoming virtually absent.

The guys sat cattycorner across from Raven, and both of them had asked the woman several times if anything strange had happened lately, or at all, and for some reason the elderly woman acted like everything was fine... And now the woman lounging in a worn-out recliner next to the three of them babbled on her about the sins of the world. Raven felt the sins she talked about, homosexuality and pornography, were in fact sins, but her attitude and the way the woman expressed her beliefs rubbed Raven the wrong way. The newly-teenager was tired and annoyed. She just wanted to confirm that there was indeed a Ghost here and then figure out what to do so they could get back on the road.

But so far the woman only talked about the news and how bad the world was; *blah blah blah blah.* Raven was nineteen now, but she had lived approximately a thousand years, and throughout those years she learned that there would always be bad and good people. Granted, some years of the world's history were worse, but some were also better. It was what it was.

After their hostess poured Raven a second glass of sweet-tea and set the jug down on the coffee table, brown water suddenly erupted out of the kitchen sink like a fire-hose at full power. Then the water turned red and thickened and overflowed onto the floor before it ceased spewing all over the kitchen wall.

The three guests knew without a doubt it was blood.

Leon and Lucas were confused but perversely calm. Raven, however, was very much perturbed and on edge; she knew what *Ghost* really meant and how quickly this matter could escalate into a dangerous situation. But she was also thrilled about being one more step closer to getting in the car and forgetting about this dead and invisible being as well as the gray haired woman sitting across from her.

"Is there anything strange now, lady?" Raven nearly slammed her drink down on the table in front of her.

"Other than what you're doing with these boys?" the extremely judgmental woman snickered. The three of them knew exactly what their hostess was implying. She was insinuating Raven was a whore.

Before Leon or Lucas could stop her Raven quickly snapped back. "And AC/DC is the devil," and then followed up by singing a verse to the shocked woman. *"Hells Bells!"* When Raven was finished the woman threw her wrinkled little hand over her mouth and Raven turned and stormed out of the house. Leon stayed behind to try to get more Ghost info from the woman and smooth things over while Lucas went after Raven. "Something tells me you aren't usually like this with people—people who need help. It seemed like you were dancing on the line of torturing her back there."

"The lady has bong-water coming from her sink! And still, she's in denial."

"So? Leaving her is the answer? Is this how the old Raven handled things?" he retorted, and she gave him a very heated, taken aback look before she slid next to Mozart in the backseat of the car and closed the door.

Lucas leaned down to reason with her, but Raven stared him dead in the eyes through the open window and retaliated with the one question he was never expecting to be asked. "Was leaving me the way you did in Kansas the answer, Kale?" Lucas winced inside and walked off, heading back to the ghost infected house.

Raven was just looking for a way to shoot Lucas down and get rid of him—she hoped he wouldn't figure it out. He was talking about the *old* Raven. Not the Raven *now*. And she wanted very little to do with the 'old' Raven. The former Goddess wanted to forget… And she was terrified of fighting ghosts and didn't want Lucas talking her into *anything*; facing that Ghost, or the ghost of herself… And he very well could have right then.

Since there wasn't really anything to do, Raven decided to walk her dog while she waited for the Vampire Hunters to come back out and ask her for the 4-1-1 on the paranormal. "Any ideas on what we are supposed to do with not so friendly Casper?" Leon finally asked as the four of them arrived back at the vehicle simultaneously.

Raven didn't know how to tell them, so she just decided that the best place to start was at the beginning. "Not all ghosts are bad. They are people who have died, who have yet to be accepted into Heaven or Hell," she explained while dropping back down onto the seat after Mozart. Raven retrieved her bag of green and joints from her satchel. "When did you get *that*?" Leon asked surprised. "Nevermind that," she said dismissively and put one of the joints to her lips and lit it. The two guys stepped back as smoke rolled out the car.

"They lived their life in the gray area," she continued. "Their sins and good deeds weigh the same. So their afterlife is purgatory—waiting—*that's a ghost*. Waiting to be judged. They need to do something to tip the scale. First action—either way. A poltergeist is a Ghost who still can't face the fact there's a God, so they torture the person they love the most that they lived with, or whoever moves in—tipping the scale…"

"To what?" Luke asked.

Looks of remorse and pity flashed through

Leon's sapphire blue eyes, taking it all in. "Hell," he answered his cousin.

"First, you have to figure out why he is torturing her. And good luck with that because according to her she doesn't have a problem. And then you have to get the mean woman to also forgive said poltergeist," Raven explained.

"Wouldn't they be judged right away? After tipping scale?"

"God's very busy. Purgatory doesn't rank high on the list. But when forgiveness is granted, the poltergeist is immediately sent away... And yes, you can be hurt by them. But not killed. That I know of. And by the way, I'm not fighting it," Raven told them. "I'm just the messenger. Ghost delivered." She took a long drag from her joint.

"Come on. It can't be that bad."

"Yeah. Leon will use his charming self to convince the old lady."

"I'll what?"

"Since you two don't believe it's that bad," she said still smoking, "then I'm sure you can take care of it." Without arguing, the guys went back inside. The lady wouldn't admit that she had a problem so Raven immediately didn't like her. And then she remembered something that she had once heard—usually the faults you find in others are the ones you dislike most about yourself... She immediately ended her thoughts, and within an hour Raven finished smoking and took Mozart for another walk, longer this time, through the small neighborhood which he seemed to enjoy very much. He tried catching a butterfly but it was too fast for him.

Afterwards, they went back to the car and Raven hopped in the front and turned the radio on. Song after song played. Bored, Raven took a break from fiddling with the radio and looked back just in time to witness Lucas and Leon practically leaping out the front door of the old lady's house. When they saw the Chevy, and her seeing them, they tried to play it cool like nothing happened. Raven didn't know whom they thought they were fooling. They could try and act like they weren't scared as hell but their faces, covered in tiny scratches, were the worst liars Raven had ever seen. She laughed all the way to the backseat. When the two of them joined her in the car their eyes were still wide—clearly spooked.

The older cousin's birthday was coming up in two days and Raven thought she would cheer them up by giving Lucas his present. She had been contemplating when to give it to him and now seemed like an opportune time. Raven casually slide it out of her satchel. "Happy birthday!" she exclaimed, handing the twenty-four year old a magazine and three tickets to Las Vegas. *"Vegas!"* Lucas shrieked. "And she got me a Playboy." He smiled at Leon.

"Can't go wrong there," the long-haired brunette observed.

"Usually."

"What does that mean?" Leon scowled.

"Dude. You rarely look at nudity."

"*Rarely* still means I do."

The gifts easily calmed them down from their terrifying experience, and Raven was satisfied. But from them being soothed by her, or from the successful diversion from facing her fears, she wasn't clear on...

LEON

Leon was a ball of laughter when he got off the phone with his uncle. Lana, Cricket, and Loki had been doing research and helping Rachel out with the farm animals: chickens, cows, and pigs. Apparently the animals didn't like Loki and they gave her a hard time. That was music to the veterinarian's ears; Leon believed animals could sense things about people. Luke even chuckled when he told him about the pigs ramming Loki's shins and the rooster that flogged her.

They pulled up the driveway to their house and Leon was still grinning from ear to ear he was so overjoyed from the news. He turned around in his seat, expecting to see a reaction of amusement from Loki's not-so-favorite-person, but instead found Raven still sleeping. The recently turned Human passed out right after the three of them left the haunted house in Adams, Tennessee.

After Lucas shut the engine off, Leon opened her door and tried to wake the sleeping beauty but she was in a deep sleep. He undid her seatbelt and wrapped her arm around his neck, intending on carrying her, but Raven began to stir. The blonde-haired girl got out, exhausted, and leaned on him for support. "I can't believe I need to downgrade my weed. I can't believe I said that," Raven yawned and fell back asleep. Lucas helped get her up the porch and to the guest bed.

The sun was setting when Cricket showed up with Rachel and Lana an hour later. The girls had made dinner for everyone. When the Hunters finished Leon decided they should get Raven up to eat too since the last meal she had was this morning. It was difficult, for both of them, but they finally managed; after shaking her like a saltshaker and repeating her name like a broken record.

I don't think it's the Maryjane making Ray this way. It's her getting used to being one of us. Human. And less than what she was. She looked so groggy during dinner... After Raven finished Leon walked her back to bed. He figured since Raven knew they were still up that she would be okay.

But she wasn't.

Mozart came back to the kitchen after Leon sat down. The dog started tugging at Cricket's leg and the African Shadow was quick to his feet. But it was too late. Raven started screaming, and when they rushed in she was already bleeding. Cricket redid the bandages from the self-inflicted scratches she had done to her body as a result of the night terrors, and he easily rocked her back to sleep. But that night the Shadow stayed by her side.

And when it came time for Leon to fall asleep, he didn't bother denying to himself that he wished he could be beside her…

May 16

Raven seemed overly concerned about her dog's health. While Luke went to his shop to prepare for his birthday trip tomorrow, Leon took Raven and Mozart to one of his clinics to check out the animal's health. As if life didn't seem strange enough to him, a guy Leon just recently met, Olsen, called Ray in the middle of his examination of the Husky. The veterinarian and the born again teenager both knew why he was calling—her test results— the ones Olsen had his doctor orchestrate while they were on his private jet to the States. Raven didn't really seem like she cared to have them done, but Olsen wasn't taking no for an answer. Leon got the impression Raven wasn't worried; she seemed fairly calm when she answered the phone.

"So I'm good then?" she asked Olsen, confirming the good news. "Thank you," she hung up cutting the conversation short, to Leon's surprise. But he let out a sigh of relief. Raven may not have been concerned but the seer, formerly The Preventer, was glad she was in excellent condition.

When Leon was finished with his patient Raven looked intently into the young vet's eyes. "Mozart is fine, right?" she asked, her voice steady. But the certified genius noticed how her retinas grew bigger... Leon was only twenty-two but he was highly educated, and he knew by the teenager's body language she was more worried about her dog than herself. "He's great, Raven. And he was the best patient I've ever had."

Raven suddenly confessed she was worried

about Mozart because he's now capable of dying. The Husky was supposed to be with her until Raven died; not just a temporary death like the one back in Kansas. Her mother, the Witch, cast a spell before the Banish, and before they became enemies and Raven killed her after she turned into a Vampire; half Vampire. The spell prevented him from growing old, or passing away even.

Vampires, zombies, demon possession, and magic, Leon thought. And he knew better than to ask 'what's next?' *There's always a next.*

Mozart jumped down from the table and then it happened.

The Husky's gray and white fur turned tan and a little girl laughed as tan paws splashed about in the wet sand. Instantly Leon was on a beach somewhere. He thought he recognized the pier but nothing was in color… It was this weird sepia… The veterinarian suddenly became aware that he was still at his clinic and Raven was there with him. The image of the little girl and dog on the beach disappeared without any warning and he felt nauseous. He went to the sink, got a small white cup from the cabinet above, and filled it with water. The water suddenly tasted salty. And his hair felt wet. The seer could see the sepia colored beach houses again beyond the sand and the pier was to his left this time. Immediately, Leon knew where he was—South Carolina. He had been there before. There were hundreds of people on the sunny beach. A little blonde boy with a yellow big bird backpack punched a taller, chunkier kid in the stomach and the boy let go of the kite string. The wind blew the sweet, salty smell around and tossed the blonde boy's *Folly Beach* shark Kite and the kid cursed before taking off after it.

Leon suddenly became aware that he was holding a cup of water—a cup of normal; not salty. And that there was only one dog here in his *normal* veterinarian clinic. One dog—a husky. One person—Raven. "Are you okay?" she asked him. "You look like you're going to be sick…"

"I saw something. I don't know why, but I think I saw the past," he said confused. "Something in South Carolina… The vision's over now. I don't feel as nauseous. And I feel sane." The young man chuckled. "Like I'm back again." The blonde woman gave him a forced little half-grin and Leon realized Raven was regarding him with fidgety eyes. He didn't want to scare her any more than she was; a lot had already happened in the few short days since they met.

Leon suggested they go back to the house and wait for Lucas. They waited for a while and then Leon grew wary. "It seems to be taking longer than it should. I wouldn't think he'd still be at work…" Leon called his mechanical cousin. No answer. Raven ended up with the same results when she called the front desk and his cell phone.

"I'm driving over to Luke's shop. Stay here in case he comes back," he told Raven, and got behind the wheel of his truck and headed for the city…

RAVEN

Raven sat in the cousins' living room thinking about the weather in South Carolina. What she should wear, and if she should go… Mozart went to the window by the front door. Someone was here. Raven heard the truck, too. She got excited and nervous. She hoped it hadn't been damaged—her brother's sword; it finally arrived!

The moving company was here. She wasn't worried about one of them being a Shadow. These moving specialist were on Olsen's pay roll. But still, she picked up her hand gun from off the table and put it on top of the bookshelf that stood in between the windows and door; making it more accessible. It was a few inches taller than her so she had to stand on her tippy-toes. And then she unlocked the dead bolt. She invited the two guys inside and they delivered her dead brother's sword to her current bedroom—the cousin's guestroom. After she thanked them and walked them out she went back to her new room. She thought about how long she was would be staying here… She liked having her brother's sword where she lived. For a brief second, she thought about how he died… The brief period of anger was too much. She knew it would lead to her thinking about other things… About other people…

Raven left the sword hanging on its position on the wall and went back to the living room where she finally made up her mind about what to pack for the Palmetto State. And quickly her mind was back to Kale and his birthday. But she didn't have much time to ponder it. Mozart's ears perked up with an alertness that announced someone was here. Someone who hadn't been here before…

There was a knock at the door, and Raven had a feeling who was making an unannounced and very unwelcome appearance. And her stomach dropped. Raven opened the door and sure enough someone she didn't want to see was standing there. Long blonde curls and all. Loki. All by herself. The younger girl had been staying at Joe's. Raven was really tired of seeing Loki and just wanted her to go away. But Raven knew she couldn't be out of her life entirely… Raven had a job to do… "What do you want?" she asked.

"Are Lucas and Leon here?"

"No."

"I'll wait." Loki bumped Raven aside. The teen didn't waste time walking around and touching things; checking the place out. She was really happy and perky, and Raven very much disliked it. "Can I help you? Or did you just come for a little touchy feely? Because there's this street called Dickerson Road—" Loki saw Raven's bedroom. The door was wide open from when she hung the very old, antique sword up that belonged to her deceased brother.

Loki didn't wait for an invite and Raven couldn't stop her. Loki was in her room, in HER space. And the gray-eyed monster didn't hesitate. She went to the wall closest to the door and picked up the very thing Raven had been protecting all these years. The weapon was too heavy, and Raven watched, horrified, as the last thing she had of her brother's fell from Loki's hands. It didn't matter that there was a soft carpet padding waiting for it... The antique cracked and it cracked in places that could never be mended back together...

Raven kneeled down and picked up the severed handle. The beginning of the sword. The beginning of the cracks...

Raven's mind grew fuzzy. Loki ran by her and Raven snatched the girl's leg out from underneath her. Loki fell down and screamed...

~~~~

Chapter 5
Cracks

May 16 (Continued)

LUCAS WAS UNDERNEATH the engine of a car when Leon showed up and delivered him the not so pleasant news; his birthday trip had to be cancelled and something was wrong with the seer's visions. After finding out his lifetime dream of celebrating in Las Vegas wasn't going to happen, Lucas received a frantic phone call from Loki. She pleaded for help, insisting Raven was after her. He had no idea what was happening as Leon and him rushed back to the house.

The two young men heard what Lucas deemed horrible music blasting from inside their self-built house. When they walked in the ingress Raven was sitting in the living room with earplugs in her ears, reading a book. Meanwhile, the other teenager sat tied to a chair inside Raven's room, tape over her mouth, and was being forced to listen the bad music exploding from the radio.

When Lucas turned the music off to stop his brain from rattling, Raven explained what happened, and Leon decided it was best if Loki didn't come around for a while and she agreed to leave Joe and Rachel's and stay in a motel. But the young girl absolutely refused to go back to Nebraska without the demon cure... Lucas didn't really know what to say. The Hunter just wanted bad crap to stop happening and to get on with at least being able to celebrate his birthday in some fashion. After calling his uncle up and informing him of the chaos going on, Rachel suggested that

Lucas be the one to travel into the city and find Loki a motel to stay in for the moment. Lucas immediately became suspicious that there was a birthday bash in the works. Why else would Rachel suggest for *him* to escort Loki?

His early birthday suspicions where confirmed after Lucas checked the quiet and pouting girl into the motel. His cousin, whom he loved like a brother, called and told him to meet up with the rest of them at Uncle Joe's. Lucas walked inside his former childhood home and Uncle Joe hugged him and gave him a beer. He told him happy birthday and Leon congratulated Lucas on getting old.

"Seriously, dude. I was *this* close to Vegas," Lucas signed with his fingers and playfully punched the seer on his upper arm. Leon started poking him and lightly insulting him, and Lucas chugged his beer and the two of them started wrestling. They expected their uncle to chime in any second with, "Cut it out," or "Take it outside, boys." But instead their father figure jumped in on the action. It wasn't long before the two young men came to the conclusion they were losing the wrestling match. "Uncle," Lucas managed to say with his cheek smashed to the floor.

"Are you forfeiting?" Uncle Joe asked for clarification. "Or are you just saying my name little lady?"

"Uncle," the two cousins gasped, and their Uncle Joe hoped off their backs smiling, pleased with himself.

Lucas wiped off his saliva that was smeared to his face from being pinned awkwardly to the floor.

Raven came out of the kitchen just then, dressed in shorts and a low-cut shirt. "I hope you don't mind, Kale. Rachel said it was okay if I baked for you this year." The golden-haired girl held a cake that had a candle in the shape of the number twenty-five on top. Usually his cousin Rachel made the cake but Lucas didn't mind. *Boy am I okay with it,* Lucas thought, and Rachel handed him another birthday beer and he took a giant swig from the bottle. *I like this birthday. Raven looks so amazing standing there!* Screamed him brain and he tried not to stare.

Everyone sang happy birthday to him and Lucas loved every minute of it; especially Raven's cake. Afterwards, he received presents from his uncle, Rachel, and Leon. Then he unexpectedly got gifts from Lana and Cricket. And one Loki had given to Lana to pass on to him; which he set aside because it felt too weird to open right now.

He almost lost his mind when Raven brought out hot wings and hugged him. Right now Lucas had two favorite things: Hot wings and Raven wearing shorts with a very sexy low cut shirt. He could feel her breast pressed against his chest when she hugged him and told him happy birthday. He decided to lay off the beer until he finished eating, because it was making him feel a certain way and all he wanted to do was have the best birthday ever—with Raven. But he knew that wasn't an option.

After his birthday dinner, Raven revealed what she was thinking; she should be the only one going to South Carolina with Leon and Lucas. And the Shadows, Lana in particular should stay behind and enjoy her summer vacation—not add to the list of *things to kill after graduation.* It was settled after a very short discussion, mostly by Raven and Cricket, even though he never spoke a word. Cricket was to take Lana back with him to Amsterdam. He would show the lead Shadow around in between Vampire staking and using Olsen's resources to find a way to fix Loki's mother.

Lucas honestly didn't know if he was thrilled or worried about his chances of being alone with the recently born again teenager. At this point he couldn't decide whether or not drinking less beer was good or drinking more was the solution.

The sun was about to bring forth another Spring night as Lucas watched Rachel feeding the dogs on the porch; Uncle Joe's Rottweiler, her Boxer, and Leon's Hound—Roxy. All three dogs tend to roam through the woods from Uncle Joe's to their place. But Roxy is the only one that occasionally stays inside at night with Leon and him. Sometimes, if it's really hot out or cold depending on the season, Rachel and his uncle will let their dogs inside, but for the most part they burrow below the highly elevated porch.

Since the twenty-four year old, twenty-five tomorrow, doubted he would be the one driving to South Carolina, Lucas figured one more beer couldn't hurt…

…Blayne looked down at his phone. It was a text message from Loki. She was supposed to be staying at a motel but she took a cab back and had the driver drop her off near the neighbor's. The determined girl traveled on foot through the woods and waited at the uncle's place.

Apparently it was his and Avy's lucky day. According to the text, both of the Shadows had just left for good and didn't plan on returning to the same state, or even the same country for a good period of time. Blayne showed his new leader the message; the phone put out a tremendous amount of light as they laid with their backs on the grass in a random cow pasture.

Blayne had to admit, Avy sure was a hell of a lot different than his Vampire father, Kronos. For one, Avy had a better technique when it came to teaching Novice's how to Push. He learned while the Goddess was overseas for the funerals; Avy still referred to her as the Goddess because it seemed nothing could kill her. The eighteen year old was a real Vampire now thanks to Avy. Not only could Blayne drain his victims by using his teeth, but he could also Push—pull it right from them and through the air if he needed to. He was a true *bloodsucker*. His teeth were retractable now, but he doubted the Humans knew that. And if he simply wanted to have extra fun he could turn someone. Hopefully Raven.

Second, Blayne was positive Kronos would never have laid down in a pasture. And when the two of them first came out here, after dusk, Blayne grew very irritated with the much older Vampire when he flopped down in the middle of fat, stinky cows and just stared up at the moon and stars. They were *Vampires* for God's sake! And *he* was their *leader*! Blayne wasn't exactly sure *what* they should be doing. Something Vampire like he supposed.

But Avy patiently explained that if he wanted to survive, *truly* survive, you had to appreciate something other than your food and controlling others. For Avy, it was the stars and the moon; not only did such beautiful light not hurt them, even though the moon's light was really a reflection from the sun, it was a kind of art that made him *even want to live forever*. He explained that while this art seemed to last forever, parts of it were already dead (stars that had burned out but would take centuries or longer for the light to finally stop reaching Earth) and it was a reminder to him that although he seemed like God it's possible for him to "burn out".

After giving the Shadows plenty of time to put some distance between the house and the others, they didn't want to be tracked, Blayne followed Avy's lead and stood up. Avy's hair had grown back, it was longer than Blayne's and a couple shades darker. Avy had told him there was no need in shaving his head because he didn't plan on being seen by anyone that mattered; the Hunters.

The nightwalkers jumped over a couple of cows as if they were playing leap frog before jumping the electric fence. They passed the farm house and soon they went from the middle of nowhere to the edge of nowhere. The Vampires stood back at the edge of the woods and watched everyone inside the house; the one that belonged to the human called Joe.

Five minutes had gone by and still Blayne hadn't been informed on what the entire plan was; he only knew the one part—the part he came up with and that wasn't occurring tonight… "Why don't we just bust in there and do it now?" he asked impatiently.

"Raven has unleashed an undetermined amount of change in the world," Avy explained sagely, "and I want to see the goodies first."

Blayne knew Avy and him were the only two, the only ones, right now that could do this; see the goodies. Avy knew for a fact that the other Shadows and Vampires didn't know the former Goddess was alive and he wanted to keep it that way. Avy said she was too controversial and they needed to execute this plan carefully. The only other Vampire—at least he thought she was a Vampire—that knew about Raven was Silhou. And she didn't want Raven to know she had been hanging around. All the secrecy confused Blayne and made him feel degraded because he wasn't seen as trustworthy enough to be let in on their agenda.

The young Vampire saw Raven and the others moving inside the house. Most of the lights were on and anyone could see through the open curtains—his Vampire eyes, now fully developed with violet around the orange pupils and irises, only made things clearer. Raven was headed for the door. The other Humans right behind her; Lucas, Leon, and a girl they had never seen before with dark hair as long as Raven's.

Avy told him to charge after Raven once her feet touched the grass, and Blayne's eagerness was like that of a hunter aiming a weapon at his prey and Blayne couldn't wait to fire. Raven opened the door and the others came outside with her—including the dog they had seen in Kansas when Blayne was weakening the Werewolf with silver spikes so his elders could rip him apart; especially his head.

The Husky took one sniff of the air and leaped off the porch, which extended all the way around the house, landing in front of Raven as soon her foot hit the grass. Immediately the dog started acting strange, pawing at his nose, like something was causing him discomfort.

"Inside!" Raven shouted, and the two guys and the girl they had never seen before didn't hesitate. They ran back up the porch without questioning her. But Blayne managed to snag the girl by her long hair before she could make it back to the porch. He spun Raven around and punched her in the face.

Blayne felt canine teeth hit his ribs.

The Husky had jumped up and took a fairly big bite out of his side. Raven started up the porch, bleeding from the nose. Blayne swatted the dog and it yelped in pain as he sent the little beast through the air. The gray and white dog crashed to the ground and didn't move. Raven stopped running and whipped around; her eyes exploded in sheer panic.

Panic Avy dearly noted from his spot hidden in the dark woods. His protégé was just about to make another start for Raven when three dogs came dashing out from underneath the wooden porch; exiting from the sides, their paws pounding like wild wolves.

Sure they were three angry and vicious looking dogs, but he was all Vampire—not a Novice. He wasn't a newborn anymore. Blayne let the Hound, Rottweiler, and Boxer come for him.

But Blayne wasn't prepared for the fire sensation ripping through his skin. Those dogs weren't just shredding his skin like a meat grinder—whatever was in their saliva made it easier for them to take out deep chunks of his skin. And whatever he had been infected with seemed to sting out from the bites—causing him severe pain and agitation. While he was momentarily distracted, Raven hurried in the pet's direction. The Husky rolled over and stood up, and ran to her. The two of them sprinted past Blayne throwing the other pursing dogs into the pig field.

From inside the house, Rayne, Mozart, Leon, Lucas, Rachel, and Uncle Joe watched the injured Vampire as he scrambled back on his feet. "Call them off before I *kill* them," he warned, the dogs were quickly making their way back to the Vampire.

Leon snickered and Lucas laughed at him, but Raven whispered, *"Get them in the house."*

"We are sitting duck—," Rachel started but Raven cut her off. *"In the house!"* She whispered loudly. Uncle Joe whistled and the dogs adverted Blayne and came bolting inside the house through the front door that was standing wide open.

Blayne didn't feel so well.

"I see you got all your eye colors. How'd ya like those doggy bites, Vampire Boy?" Lucas taunted. "You'd be surprised what a little holy water and dead man's blood will do when mixed together in a dog's diet." He smiled. "You know…at the hospital your old pops wanted Raven to admit some great secret. That she killed a human. Well…my cousin

Leon and I have a secret of our own."

"During our quest for a Vamp named Avy Sinanna, we may have gotten a little rough a time or two," Leon confessed.

"That's right." Lucas nodded. "We know all about Vampire torture. And right now I'm thinking you're the kind that cracks. Like a little egg. So tweet tweet little birdie. Come to daddy." His lips turned into a half-smile and he held up a crossbow.

Blayne's anger ignited like a grill bursting into flames and he jumped up on the porch; without a single idea what his move should be. Rip their heads off. That seemed like a start.

Not sure what Raven had in mind, Lucas Kale prepared to release his arrow into the bloodsucker's heart. Suddenly, Blayne acted as if he hit something they couldn't see, like someone accidentally running into a glass door. The dark-haired Vampire started convulsing and foaming at the mouth like he was having one massive seizure.

"It's like he's being electrocuted," Rachel observed, standing beside her father.

"That's exactly it," Raven confirmed, smiling. "I thought the rules had changed. Before, Vampires could go into any house without an invitation, but now… Sorry, little birdie. This nest is full," she told Blayne and closed the door.

From the edge of the woods, Avy Sinanna quietly called for the Vampire kid. He bit into his own flesh and gave the younger, wounded Vampire some of his blood to fight off the infection inside him. Holy water was bad. Having a dead man's blood in your system was really bad. But having both seemed to be extremely worse. Avy's old and powerful blood was healing the kid, but not as fast as the Vampire would have liked. And he knew it wasn't wise to be out here any longer. "Let's go," he whispered, throwing Blayne's arm over one shoulder. Blayne Vandor painfully limped through the woods with Avy Sinanna...

...After the unexpected appearance from Blayne, Lucas immediately went to the kitchen and got a beer. Raven sat down on Uncle Joe's couch and started to hyperventilate from shock; from how much pain she was in and how she did nothing to stop Blayne. Rachel handed her a tampon to put in her nose to absorb the blood. "It's going to be so easy for him to tear me apart," Raven said in between breaths. Lucas handed her a brown paper bag and told her to breath into it. He sat down next to her and rubbed her back while taking big gulps from his Bud Light; nearly halfway finished.

Raven breathed into the bag a couple times. But when Mozart limped by and laid down, she threw the bag to the ground and kneeled beside him. She was going to pet him, to comfort him, but then she became afraid that she would hurt him. Leon kneeled to the floor to examine the Husky. Raven got up and headed outside, pulling the tampons out from her nose. "Ray, he might still be out there," Lucas cautioned.

"I think Mozart's going to be fine," Leon called out but Raven headed out the door anyway, worrying all of them.

Lucas quickly downed the rest of his beer and sat

the empty bottle on the coffee table before he calmly went out the back door. Raven flung the tampons into the backyard and paced back and forth. She snapped out of her trance for a brief second when Lucas stepped in her path and put his hands on her shoulders. But then she resumed back to breathing irregularly. The hazel-eyed girl pulled away from him and sat down on the porch. "My dog, my dog. The house, the house." Raven rocked back and forth. "How did he find us?"

"Raven, stop!" The young man said loudly and sat down beside her and pinned her against his chest; stopping the rocking. Lucas pulled her blonde hair back from her face and gently stroked her head; his fingertips just barely brushing through her hair. For a moment it seemed to work; he brought her back from whatever place she was slipping into. But the moment disappeared as quickly as it had come and her breathing grew shorter and faster.

The back porch light flicked on and the backdoor opened. Lucas was surprised when Leon walked out carrying a bowl and a lighter; Rachel's bowl that was meant for smoking weed. "Normally, I don't agree with this… But here." He sat down next to them and put the bowl to Raven's lips and lit it for her. Raven inhaled a couple times and then coughed.

Raven's mind became less fuzzy and her breathing slowed down. She took the lighter from Leon and lit the bowl again. The herb smelled wonderful to her. She inhaled again, relaxing. "It's okay," Leon reassured her. "I know," she said and looked down at her feet.

"So that's where PJ went," Rachel nodded, coming outside. "PJ?" Raven asked. "Pajama. That's my before bedtime bowl," Rachel told her and lit the joint she was holding.

"I didn't know where hers was, so I grabbed yours, Rach," Leon admitted.

"You normally smoke?" Rachel asked, joining them and passed the joint to Raven. Loki had said a lot of bad things about the blonde-haired chick. But Rachel was starting to like Raven more and more. She knew about the incident with her brother's sword and she felt bad. And now, sharing a certain herb, Rachel decided Raven wasn't so bad. The two of them smoked the entire joint together, and Lucas had another beverage.

After saying goodbye to Rachel and Uncle Joe, Lucas called shotgun and Raven climbed in the backseat with Mozart. Leon, the only sober one, got behind the wheel of the car and they began the eight hour drive to South Carolina...

* * *

Present

I awake to the sound of nothing. The TV is turned off, and a small lamp in the kitchen is the only light that's on in the house. I must have drifted off during HALLOWEENTOWN. The popcorn, pizza, and beer have already been cleared off the coffee table. I realize Leon's seat is empty and instantly I feel alone. The feeling sickens me. And my heart literally stops when Mozart comes inside from the doggy door Leon installed for him and Roxy after Raven died.

Mozart refused to go back with Olsen, so Leon has been taking care of him while I do my best to avoid him. I rush back to my room to read Leon's journal. Right now my cousin's is probably the only one I can read from without tearing up. And if I try to sleep I know I will end up crying and I *definitely* don't want to do *that*. I prop the pillows behind me and kickback on my bed and begin reading.

The next three weeks. SC.

We spent hours and days and days searching/researching for answers.

(We did that was true. We got our hotel room, that Raven insisted on paying for, and then spent the next couple of weeks or so away from our normal lives mostly doing nothing but boring research. And hunting Ghosts. Charleston just seemed to be sprouting poltergeists up all over the place. I figured it would be some place like Louisiana. And by all over the place I mean three. To some people I guess this wouldn't seem like a lot, but dealing with three dead-ghost-people-things, one after the other was actually a little scary. These were all in the first week and we still couldn't find any information on Demons and possession.

Raven was seeing the present, but not just mean and scary poltergeists. One time we were speeding and she saw a cop parked ahead of us, way ahead and out of sight. I don't know why she saw that…but it saved me from getting a speeding ticket so I wasn't complaining.

And I still have no idea what's going on with Leon. His visions are few and far in between and he wasn't seeing much. Well not like he used to. Not even as of late. I remember all of us thinking that God was the only one who could see the future now since neither of them received images from the future like they used to. Leon talked about his first vision of the Demon we were hunting while we were in the car. He said his vision was odd, strange, and scary, but something was familiar. Raven told us Demons created the Vampires. More specifically Satan did. He created the first Vampire. That somewhere it says the Devil can't create living things—well Vampires aren't technically *living*. "That's what you were feeling…the familiar feeling of evil in your visions," I remember her saying. Her voice was so sweet and more beautiful than snow.

Raven still had night terrors if she slept by herself so we stopped trying. I rather enjoyed her company at night—not sleeping beside her. I thought it best not to. As a result, Leon spooned with her when it was time to sleep. I only did it twice.

And a couple of times I left her and Leon at whatever bar we chilled at to score with a female—I actually remember their names. When the second week and round of watching Raven and Leon spoon together at night came, there was a lot going on in my head and I couldn't sort it out. And I was itching to kill a Vampire.

I preferred to stalk a vamp named Blayne for helping Kronos and the Devil in turning us humans into zombies and forcing Raven's hand; uncaging the Demons. I would have also taken anyone named Avy. He took something that didn't belong to him. My family. Only now it was harder since Leon wasn't seeing them in the future—the Vampires. And it wasn't like I knew any Shadows down there. I just found out about their existence; the same day that Nebraska and Kansas became a land of zombies. A great deal of the Shadows died when we were caught up in some intense seriousness between

Raven and the Vampires. And the battle with the zombies.

But I did manage to kill a Novice while we were down there. The challenge turned out to be the best thing for me—it was the best release. But it was also the most dangerous. Stalking a Vampire wasn't an easy thing to do anymore. After I was finished I felt powerful though as I strolled through the streets at night on my way back to the motel. The spring air was warm. But the breeze from the Charleston Harbor lightly played with the Spanish moss trees and made it feel as though some sort of magic was in the air; a good kind.

Spanish moss trees…Raven…

I snap out of memory lane. I looked down at my cousin's journal again and start over. I want to read *his* memories. Not relive mine.)

The next three weeks. SC.

We spent hours and days and days searching/researching for answers. How to get a Demon out of someone…? We didn't know truth from fiction. As a result, Loki ended up sticking around.

(Oh, yeah. She stowed herself in the trunk before we left Tennessee and tossed all of our clothes out so she could fit.)

Yay us. And apparently she's book smart. Free ride to college. Loki said her dad felt guilty for leaving her with her mom so he had set some money aside for her to do whatever she wanted after her high school graduation. Which doesn't make sense to me. Instead of paying her off, why didn't he just take his daughter back to live with him before graduation? I'm done trying to figure out the insanity that involves Loki. She lives up to her name. Where there's Loki, there's <u>trouble</u>. I hate the fact that she was staying in my old room at my Uncle's. But I guess she really doesn't have anywhere to go.

Loki was only with us for a week though. Her and Ray made it clear they are enemies, the constant insults—Raven's more clever. Loki tried to flirt with me, but I just ignored her. She flirted with Luke, too. He tried his best to not be alone with her but she intentionally found ways. She made him horny but as far as I know he has never did anything with her. Loki was satisfied that she turned Luke on, but most girls turn Luke on.

My cousin will eventually make some sort of romantic commitment to someone, but it won't be Loki. It's whether or not Lucas loves you that is something to be proud of. I just wonder what happens when Loki's childish game is forced to end?

B.L.C

I put Leon's thoughts down and I back myself against the wall that my bed is against. I thought about those few weeks with Ray. Things were hard for me—in more ways than one. And I didn't want to be around her. The less I liked about Raven the better, I figured.

I had to avoid a lot of situations. Like going with Leon and Mozart and her to the beach when we weren't Demon hunting. I was making all kinds of excuses to not be around Raven. I only went to the beach three times; twice because I had to on account of Leon's visions, and the other time I waited for them to leave and then I took a cab to Folly Beach. Ray never knew I was there. I did see her from a distance though. She was having fun. She and Leon were sitting close together on a blanket they had spread out on the sand. She smiled and my cousin fed her a Vienna sausage. That seemed to be her new favorite thing now that—*she was human.* My train of thought is shot and instantly my memory of her is shattered. And the happy feeling that kept me alive is pulled out from underneath me again like Aladdin's magical carpet. Only there is nothing magical about feeling this alone, this sad, this depressed. This fucking everything that I can't stand.

I flip open my stupid journal and practically carve the words with my pen.

October 7

It's been a week since I saw her. And two days since her funeral.
It's still October.
Raven's still gone.
And I still don't feel the least bit better.

I get up and open my window. I stand there staring out into the darkness. The chilly air is slowly beginning to replace what used to be a warm and soothing season. I go back and turn off the light. I just stand there for a moment, staring out into absolute darkness. I hear the October wind as it comes to claim the leaves that once were so alive. Feeling around, I shove whatever journals or diaries I touch to the floor, not really caring if they get damaged, and I get underneath my covers.

~~~~

Chapter 6
South Carolina

MAY

It's not just my senses that have changed. It's changing. Changing fast. Changing slow. Ageing. Moving. Sitting. Thinking. Everything. Touch. Breathing.

Breathing. I remember it's what I focused on at their funerals. But eventually I will grow accustomed to this...

My Orders. I wonder if I still even have them? Something strange happened to me today. I don't know if it was an Order just interpreted differently now with this...with me, or if they are gone for good and whatever this is has replaced them?

*I saw what was happening. I saw the present. The **present** of all things. And that's not the bad part. What I saw was a ghost. It looks like my fears are coming true. Awesome. Ghosts—poltergeists; ones who make the wrong choice—are going to be just one category out of many...*

So I said I couldn't go help Loki. That I must, as much I didn't want to, go deal with that freaking ghost!!! Except I was a little calmer than that. Anyway, Leon thought they should go with me and Lucas agreed with his cousin. He didn't say much but he acted like it was because he didn't want to let Leon out of his sight. Not sure why. Kale was different now. He wasn't like he was when we were in Kansas. But I guess I shouldn't expect him to be. I'm not sure where I stand with him...

So Rachel, their cousin, suggested that I stay, find out what's going on with my new "vision stuff" she called it—I like her. But I think Loki may be responsible for the standoffish way Rachel is around me. That's another topic. So Rachel said stay and help find ways to kill Demons since I'm pretty sure I wasn't given Orders... But ultimately the three of us—Kale, Leon, and myself— decided to go play with a ghost. (Sad face)

Afterwards, before I left for South Carolina, I told Cricket & Lana "They should take the summer off—enjoy their lives. Spend some time together. Just focus on any vamps in Amsterdam. It's obvious there is some connection between you two," Is what I think I said. Lana said something to me I didn't expect. "You shouldn't make big life altering decisions after someone dies..." I wasn't sure which one of us she was talking about... If I know Lana like I think I do, then she was trying to give us both advice. But it was easy for Cricket and me to convince her.

Lana called Loki—she had been taken to a motel for "accidentally" (yeah right) breaking my sword (brother's). Loki agreed with us... She told Lana she could research anywhere.

Cricket really likes her—Lana. He despises Loki. I knew he wanted Lana to get away from the madness for the time being.

"I let the Demons loose and opened the door for so many other things... I'm responsible," I told them. "My temporary death caused this."

The three of us; Lucas, Leon, and I headed towards the car, fixing to go to South Carolina when a stupid Vampire showed up!

HOME

*A stupid Vampire named Blayne. I'm freaked out about Blayne; for lots of reasons. But mostly because I haven't seen...**Him** yet. I don't have Orders, and I don't know what to do. And my memory is slipping it seems like. I have forgotten how to speak most of the languages I knew. I have forgot words. What else am I forgetting?*

I'm not sure what day it is. I think today's the Tenth of October. I went to work today as I have the past two days, but I haven't been keeping up with time. I sit down at my desk at the house and lay Ray's diary down in front of me. I pull open the desk drawer and pull out the picture Leon took of Ray and me when we the three of us were in South Carolina. I use it to save my place before I shut the diary.

Three thoughts keep my mind busy: Cricket's cryptic entry, something about Olsen and another dimension, and now some character referred to as 'Him'. Next, for some reason, I think back to when Lana, Cricket, and Leon gave me their journals and stuff. They hoped it would ease my pain. I remember my surprised reaction when I found out my cousin wrote down his feelings. He said something along the lines of, "Not every day, but yeah."

I open her diary again and flip the page over to the next entry. *Ray's dead so she won't mind...*

JUNE
Friday morning

Carmany saw the past again. Only this time it was more recent; he saw where the Demon was 30 minutes after it was there. I think that's pretty cool. So the three of us packed up and hit the beach. Isle of Palms to be exact. I WILL NEVER FORGET IT!

As usual we couldn't find that freaking Demon—what a nuisance. So I stripped down to my swimsuit and relaxed on the sandy beach. I was happy that Kale was with us for once. But not for long... I was using the restroom, like I do a million times now, when my life decided to get even stranger. I wiped and there was freaking blood on the tissue paper. WHAT THE H?

"Oh, great," I mumbled to myself. I flew out of the stall and asked a lady for a tampon or pad. She didn't have one. Yippy. I wore my shorts over my swim bottoms when

I went to the bathroom so I pulled out my phone and went through my contacts. I scrolled down, passing by Cricket, Ganesha, Jet, pausing at each one. I swallowed. Then I scrolled by Lucas and Leon and down to Olsen's phone number. I put my finger on the call button and hesitated. "What could he do?" I put the phone back in my pocket.

I then looked at myself in the mirror and sighed. "Joy." I left the bathroom and walked back to Lucas and Leon making something with the sand. Leon was probably making something cool, but who knows with Lucas. Probably boobs.

"Uh, listen, I'm not feeling well, is it cool if I borrow your wheels?"

"It would help if you borrowed the entire ride instead," Kale joked, of course. I smiled, trying to act like the world wasn't ending. And then Leon said that maybe one of them should go with me. Then the two started arguing over who should go. Truthfully I didn't want either of them going, but I knew that was an argument I was sure to loose. So I tried using the pretty half-

naked girls as a distraction and a reason to stay on Kale's part. But even that didn't work. If I wasn't so worried about blood soaking through my shorts and time being an issue, I'm sure I could have convinced him. But time was indeed running out. I just left them and headed for the car.

And of course they both came.

When we got to the store I told them to stay in the car, that I was an ex-Vampire and I didn't need a damn chaperone to get a few grocery items. Once inside the store, I thought I was in the clear and free of humiliation.

But it turns out being a teenager is really starting to suck butt.

I was inside the store for all of 20 seconds when Leon randomly popped up beside me after I passed by the vitamin aisle. "What are you doing???? You didn't have to come—"

"I'm a genius, Ray. I know what's going on. Why would you suddenly have to leave

the water to go to the store? I know all about your lady—"

And that's when I practically yelled, "I don't care!!!"

And then he told me there's nothing to be embarrassed about and I snapped at him again. "I don't know what's going on with me. But I just want you to walk away and meet me at the car like a normal <u>non-genius</u>!!!

<u>I WILL NEVER FORGET</u> Isle of Palms because I started my freaking period!!!! And during one of the few times Luke was actually with us!! Like seriously???

I feel bad for being so ridiculous. But sadly that wasn't the end of the embarrassment.

I remember this. I mark the page again and set her thoughts down. I can't stop thinking about what happened next. I pick up my pen.

INSIDE CAR

Raven missed her friends. And she was centuries old and trapped in a 19 year old body.

"You can talk to me. To us. About anything. Seriously," I told her. Raven stared at me, kinda lost looking. And then it clicked. "He told you! You told him?!" she evil-eyed Leon. "Yeah..." he admitted when Ray pulled his hair, and he threw his hands up in defense and scooted up to the dashboard. Raven sighed and threw herself back against the seat and stared straight-ahead, like she was burning a hole into some other universe.

"It shouldn't be embarrassing." I tried reassuring her. "Okay, it's not," she lied. "New subject."
"No."
"No?"
"You don't talk."
"I talk," she said and rolled her eyes.
"Not about what's going on with you."
"You mean my feelings?"
"Yeah."
"I'm confused. You're a dude. You know that, right?"

I ignored her attempt to insult me and

jumped to my point. "You haven't grieved. It's been weeks and you haven't cried or even talked about them."

Raven knew I was talking about her friends and instantly locked her jaw. "I'm fine."
"No, you're not."
"Don't tell me how I feel," she said through gritted teeth.
"That would be anger."

Raven, realizing that anger is one of the stages of the grieving process, hardcore looked into my eyes and it felt like her soul was on fire, burning with resentment. I stared back calmly. I was willing to be that water, so to speak, that made everything better and put out the fire. But she broke the death-stare match by swinging the car door open and she rushed out. I went after her while Leon stayed with the car.

"Do you want to hit me?" I asked her, walking a few feet behind her, passing cars in the lot. The hot South Carolina sun beating down on us. "Would that make you feel better?" I could feel her rolling her eyes again. She stopped walking. "The fact that you asked such a question makes me want to."

"You're my best friend." I randomly confessed. I hadn't know her for long, but it

was the god's honest truth. She whirled around and faced me. "What?"

"Leon is like a brother to me...and you, you're my best friend." I slowly and cautiously walked closer to her. I wasn't sure what she would do—run off or kick me in the nuts. "Sometimes I don't understand what you are saying, Ray, but the parts that I understand make sense." She let out a tiny laugh, and I smiled. "You laughing because to understand is to make sense, so of course the parts that I understand make sense?"

She nodded in agreement, laughing a little more. I hugged her. Her hair was basically dry now from the heat and it smelt like the sun. It was wonderful. "That's my girl." I put my left hand on her lower back and my right hand at the base of her head. Her blonde hair was so soft. She was in my arms. Then I had loved it. I knew she was runnin' from something, her feelings or what have you, but she wasn't running away from me— even though she should have. Yet for the moment she was in my arms and Raven was safe and sound.

Underneath all the bullshit that is me, that's all I've ever wanted.

HOME

That wonderful long hair of hers that smells so wonderful to me—that used to—now that beautiful fragrance does nothing but torture me as I pick up my pillowcase and sniff it. The pillowcase she slept on before she…

Raven slept in my bed the night before she died. On September Thirtieth Leon was on call at one of his vet clinics, and because Raven was still having night terrors and nothing but human companionship could prevent them, I let her sleep in my bed with me.

Anger's upon me again.

I figure the best way to fix it is to burn everything on my bed; the sheets, the pillowcases. I grab it all and take them out back, and inhale Raven's scent one last time before I put em' in the barrel used for burning stuff. I go back inside and grab the lighter fluid and a lighter. When I get back outside the sun has almost gone down. I spray the lighter fluid in the barrel and I set the memories on fire.

By the time the fire burns out my anger has left me. And all I'm left with is an empty hole where my heart used to be.

And no sheets to sleep on.

* * *

STATEN

(June)

Past

BLAYNE

He decided to start recording events; sort of his way of trying to keep his sanity and not lose touch with this world. This was his very first entry since they left Tennessee; his first entry period. He spoke into the voice recorder. "They—Raven, Lucas, and Leon—finally managed to track down the Demon in South Carolina at the abandoned house. But it was all planned by us." Blayne felt odd talking to a piece of junk, but he smiled as he recalled the previous moments.

"The Demon, not the one with the Shadow's mom, tricked them and trapped them there. Ha ha!" He smiled. "Prior to them being trapped in that house, Avy and I met with the Demon. We knew about him because of Loki—that was what she was there for. To give us information. To be our mole. Especially since we can't go out into the sunlight. Loki hid in the trunk of the car when they left Tennessee. She only stayed with them the first week.

"But the rest of the time they didn't know about. Loki really stayed behind and planted our listening devices. We heard everything Ray and the Hunters talked about. Then we told the Demon when Raven and the Hunters were on to him and where they would be next. Avy and I have their scents now, so that is how we were able to keep track of them and where they were headed. But we kept our distance because that dog of hers can smell us; most dogs can but Raven's seems to be highly trained. The Hunters' dogs as well. And now they probably feed him that crap that screwed me up. Neither one of us wanted to test that theory. But Avy and the Demon, who wouldn't reveal his true name to me, devised a different kind of plan... Further testing her." Blayne clicked the button and it stopped recording.

The teenage Vampire sat alone in the hotel. He wondered where the new Leader of the Vampires had gone. Avy told him he needed to take care of some business. Apparently the kind that didn't include him. And that's why Blayne stole the recording device earlier from the hotel's gift shop. Avy was disappearing a lot lately and the young Vampire didn't have the slightest clue how to function on his own.

Blayne yearned to turn Raven into a Vampire; the kind of Vampire he was—void of all humanity. But he knew there was no way in hell his new surrogate daddy would let that happen any time soon. Blayne wondered what Avy was up to... If he was meeting with that freakishly weird "sixteen" year old with crazy blue hair and weird ass powers. Her walking through cave walls and shit, after she showed up with the security DVD's from Raven's, was not something he had witnessed any other vamp do. He didn't think about Silhou for long. His thoughts quickly shot back to Raven. *What was she doing right now on this Friday night?*

* * *

JUNE
Friday afternoon

We finally tracked that annoying Demon to some old abandoned house in SC that was by a swamp and surrounded by Cypress and Spanish-moss trees. It felt like some straight up Anne Rice crap; Louisiana, Louis and Lestat living by a swamp. (Not that Rice writes crap.) We made sure to steer clear of the alligators whose eyes shined bright with intimidation when our flashlights beamed upon them. A scary intimidation I'm sure I once bestowed upon humans—and Vampires—in what seems like a lifetime ago.

We thought we had the Demon from Leon's vision trapped. After all, there were only two doors and three of us. And plus the windows were boarded up. But then he disappeared behind that stupid bookshelf and then that's when things really got fun. Lucas and I ran straight into an invisible wall that turned green and knocked us back against the far side wall. That felt awesome. (Sarcasm).

We discovered we were trapped inside, after multiple attempts at throwing whatever we could find at the doors and boarded up windows. The same stupid wall popped up. I was so mad. I knew what it was. A freaking spell. And spells can only be cast by witches. I don't know whom that thing is working with, but I don't like it. I especially don't like it that witches are back. Due to the fact that I had to kill my own mother because of what she did with her magic.

I knew there was only one way out of the house, and the whole time I felt nauseated by what I feared. Even before we paid attention to the candle and piece of paper that had been placed for us to find on the cloth covered table in the room with the "bookshelf". Leon shined his light over the letter and then said, "We need a virgin to light the candle."

"I don't know any virgins," Lucas admitted, astonished. "Or any available and here right this second." I picked up the black candle. My hands shaking. After the beach I began to wonder... I struck the

lighter, held the flame to the all-knowing virgin wick, and took in the expressions on their faces. Kale's eyes were wide, eyebrows lifted, intrigued and he had a smile that of one lust torn, yet satisfied. Leon's eyes were softer than usual and glazed over with something... Not lust. I don't know if I would call it...lov—

Anyways, I don't know what it was, and I knew before ever even looking down at the candle that it was as I feared... After the beach incident I had begun to wonder... There was a flame but not one known to me; the fire burned whiter than snow. And the edges of the flame seemed to be sending out tiny pink glowing and sparkling glittery things.

"As if life wasn't weird enough already," I said to the guys, and sat the freaky "candle" back down. This whole experience was making me uncomfortable. And then the thing started turning white and thickening like it was white chocolate and then red light exploded from it blinding me—us...

I more than knew what happened that Friday night—I was there, and I was curious as to what she had written, but there wasn't anything... So I lay down on my new sheets. I tried sleeping on the couch last night after I destroyed the only comforter set I had, but Mozart came inside and laid down in my line of sight. He looked so innocent sleeping there on the floor in his bed. But he reminded me of Raven and I just wasn't ready to be around him so I got up, got in my truck, and headed to the only twenty-four hour store near me that supplied bed stuff. I got my sheets and some beer, and got out because the place was stocked with Halloween junk. Halloween would be over in about three weeks and if I could just make it through this month I would survive. I had a few drinks when I got back because I knew the shop was closed today and then I went to bed.

I watch the blades on my ceiling fan spin around, listening to it make this clicking noise that sounds like the world's fastest clock; tick tick tick tick. My phone rings and I pull it out of my pocket. It's Rachel. I don't answer. I just want to reminisce about that hot Friday night in June when we were still in South Carolina.

We were in the car, parked at a plantation. I brought her there because it seemed like a good make-out spot. I was torn between dating her and telling her it could never happen. I decided to make up my mind when I got there. We were looking at the trees, covered in Spanish moss that dripped down to the ground like thick green spider webs. And the stars were so bright. I wanted to kiss her so badly; which is exactly what I thought. I put my hand on her face and I kissed her. She kissed back. Heavily. Before I knew it, my arm was around her waist and she was in my lap. She was wearing a skirt. Her tongue felt good against mine. *But it always feels good,* I suddenly thought. *I've been in this situation lots of times. And always going further than kissing. I've had girl after girl in this vehicle.* And then I knew the answer. *I can't take her virginity and then leave her. I'm not* that *cruel.*

"I can't do this," I said. "I've been going back and forth trying to decide what's best—a first. I know what I said to you on that rooftop, but I can't have a romantic relationship with you. The best I can offer is friendship."

Raven's hands softly dropped from my face to my chest, gently resting there as her hazel eyes calmly stared into my own. "Okay," she said with an acceptance that surprised me. She didn't even ask why.

"Okay?"

"Yeah," she said getting off of me and settling back in her seat. "I know it's nothing I did. Your penis told me what a *hard* decision it was."

I chuckled. "Did you really just say that?"

"So, now what are we going to do? I don't want to go back."

"I brought something just in case." I opened the glove box and pulled out a joint.

"Wow," Raven laughed. "Works for me."

I could tell she wasn't expecting that. And then I did the last thing she expected. I put the joint to my lips and lit it. I heard her gasp. "Don't tell Leon, okay?" I said after I exhaled, passing it to her feeling just like a teen again. Not wanting to be 'tattled' on. "K," she replied and took a hit. The way the joint was in between her fingers, touching her soft lips, it really made me want to be near them again.

She passed the jay back to me. "What about a shotgun?" I suggested.

"Lucas, I am nineteen and horny **and** I'm smoking marijuana, which makes me even more turned on. If your lips come anywhere near mine I'm going to rape you."

My eyebrow raised and I could feel my eyes getting bigger. As did my penis. *I am a horny twenty-five year old guy alone with a hot and horny nineteen year old virgin and we both are smoking weed. What have I done?* I silently asked myself as I rolled down the window and the smoke rolled out. I started the Biscayne, turned the head lights on, and did a doughnut just for fun. Then we headed out of the plantation.

I liked Raven. It was this reason that I wanted her to live. She had been given a full human life. I didn't want to be the one to take it away from her. Only I did…

I bet Leon wrote something about that weekend. I snatch his journal up off the floor and quickly flip it open. I was right.

June
Saturday night

Raven was dancing.

Luke and I went to the club Ravin' Raven's the last week we were there. Raven owns the franchise so we decided to check it out since we were down there in SC. We got our ID's checked at the door, like normal people. The inside was nice. It was aquarium style—with real fish swimming up and down glass poles from the floor and up to the ceiling.

People were taking shots; mostly smoking hot females, but the crowd wasn't necessarily thin on males. There were several bars set up. Men and women passed around jello shots. There didn't seem to be a shortage of booze. Luke surveyed the females; as usual. Smiles covered his face. Clearly he was very pleased with tonight's crowd of women. I could tell he was trying to figure out which honey he wanted to spend the night with from the outstanding selection. We walked over to one of the bars; the less slammed out of the five and ordered beers. Everything was good until Lucas looked at the crowd.

Luke went to take another big swig of his beer and froze. I looked over at the dance floor to see who or what held my cousin's intense gaze. Dancing in the middle of the club...there she was. I immediately found Raven in her red high-heels, bare legs, decent length black skirt, and dark red patterned shirt that exposed the perfect amount of her perfectly tanned skin. Her hair was beautifully curled and spiraling down around her boobs and gorgeous face. But she wasn't alone. Three guys danced around Raven. I could tell Luke didn't like how close they were to Ray. They were nearly all over her.

The average-looking guy dancing behind her wrapped his arm around Raven's exposed stomach and that's when Lucas gets up; intending on going over there and breaking it up. I put my hand on Luke's shoulder. "Dude, what are you doing? You can't go over there acting like the jealous ex-boyfriend. Because you aren't." He realized I was right. "And what are you getting so worked up for? YOU broke it off before it even started," I reminded him.

"Man... I don't know, Brighton." He sat back down and chugged his beer. Luke began flirting with our bartender, of course. I glanced out and saw Ray looking in our direction. She left the group of guys. And weaving through the crowd of dancing bodies she came over to Luke and me. And that's when things went to hell. I don't know what Lucas was thinking. But he really needs to get a grip.

B.L.C

I slam his journal shut and leave it on the bed. I pass by my desk, the dresser, and closet as I go over to my window and throw open the curtains. The sun is bright, but nothing like it was this past summer. My Biscayne is gone. I don't remember when, maybe the other day, but I finally had someone come and get it. Since it was beyond repair, I figured there wasn't much use in keeping it. I can't believe it's gone. Just like her... My best friend.

I'm upset. But not at my cousin. He wasn't wrong. I was very much in the wrong that night...

"Hey!" Raven said, and Leon smiled and said hey as she popped up on the other side him. He extended his left arm around her waist, hugging her. It seemed Leon hugged her whenever he happened to see her. She didn't seem to mind. "Nice club," he complimented.

"Hey," I said, I was clearly surprised to see she had joined us at the bar. Placing a Bud Light down in front of me, the bartender asked Ray what she wanted. "Long Island," Ray answered her employee. "What do you think?" she was asking me about her club. "I, huh," I had been so distracted by the amount and kind of attention Raven was getting, and how hot she was dressed, that her question threw me off. Apparently I came across as not liking it because that's exactly how she took it.

"Well, that's okay. It can't be everyone's thing." What she said reminded me of how the boys danced with her and I responded with, "Unlike you." I know what I said was out of line, but I wanted to feel better and it was an easy fix. Raven looked like she was about to fall to pieces. Then out of nowhere *he* showed up.

Olsen Courtney. "Hey stranger, can I get a dance?"

The bartender handed Raven her Long Island. "Always," she told Olsen. And to me, she said, all composed, "I'm sorry you feel that way," and walked away; arms entwined with his. I was mad. Mad that I was proud of Raven for the way she handled my ignorant ass and very pissed that I drove her right out onto that dance floor with that smug bast—this next moment I'm not proud of.

I took a sip of my beer—a BIG sip, and Leon got up and said something like, "I think we should leave, Lucas." Leon's eyes instantly drifted to Raven. I didn't know what was happening out on that dance floor—I didn't want to know. But I sure as hell wasn't *ever* letting the two of them out of my sight. So I decided to stay and do the one thing I'm good at. I turned to the babe who just sat down next to me. "Hey," she started the conversation off all sexy like. She obviously liked what she saw. For a moment I was into her, but then I started thinking about Raven. I turned again and saw Ray resting her head against the side of his face. *Olsen.* Jealousy definitely tore through my flesh and bones. It took my soul and tortured it. Worst of all, when I recalled the way he treated me at Ganesha's, Sheba's, and Jet's memorial service I let the jealousy consume me. I was up, off that barstool.

"Lucas—" Leon started.

"I'm just going to talk to him." I was out on the dance floor in less than three seconds. "Why are you here?" I demanded from Pretty Boy Olsen, butting in on their dancing.

"I'm here to see Raven. Do you have a problem with that? Scratch that I don't care."

"Do you *care* for *her*?"

"Of course. That's why I'm here. Now can you give us a moment or do you have any more hypocritical insults that you would like to share?" He brought up my douche baggery towards Raven at the bar and I just… She was standing there, beautiful as ever of course. I knew she was hurt and that she was controlling her emotions. And I knew that because I'm the one who hurt her. And Olsen just had to bring it up. He just had to remind her. Remind me. Remind me of how much of a screw up I was. Was he really any better than me? I punched him in the mouth. Raven gasped, and security was on me quicker than a fly on a hamburger. But I didn't much care. "You haven't seen her since May and now you suddenly show up. I've been there for her every single day," I practically shouted at him. And the music stopped.

"Lucas," Raven softly whispered my name.

"And now?" Olsen asked. "What are you doing? Besides disturbing her business and embarrassing her? Take him out," he told the bouncer holding my right side. The wickedly beefy dude started dragging me along and I told him I could walk just fine. I looked back over my shoulder, searching for Ray. I saw Olsen escorting her away from the crowd—the scene that I caused.

I'm not exactly sure what happened after that. All I know is that I had gotten kicked out of Raven's nightclub, and some of the missing pieces I was filled in on; like her coming out the back to talk to me and there was Blayne. He tried to kidnap her. She hit him and it hurt—more than she thought it would.

"You probably shouldn't do that anymore," that annoying little Vampire turd taunted her. Raven went for his eyes, but he blocked her just in time. "I'm not going to hurt you." "Yeah right! Help!!" I was about to unlock the car when I heard her scream. Leon was there and he was opening the trunk and pulling out the giant cross—basically the only thing Loki didn't toss out when she hid in the trunk.

The two of us ran back to the alley. I'm pretty sure people were wondering what the hell Leon and I were doing but we didn't really care. We found Blayne on top of her. Leon, holding the oversized cross, ran straight for Blayne. But he willingly climbed up off of her. And that's when her security guards, the ones with guns, came flying out the back door and from around the corners of the club. "I'm fine. Leave us," she ordered them and they went back inside with no questions asked about the attempted kidnapping and the guy waving a cross.

"I would be careful if I were you," Blayne pointed at the security cameras. "I would hate for you to do anything that reveals I'm a Vampire. I'm not sure how to Burn someone. Wouldn't want to have to kill your guards, Raven."

"What do you want?" she asked, highly annoyed.

"I'm getting it." His eyes gleamed Vampire—green, orange, and purple with a devilish tint to them—before he blended in with the shadows, underneath the security cameras and disappeared into the night.

Raven became horrified and frightened, realizing he truly had been doing nothing more than testing her powers, seeing if he could actually...what? Kill her? Sure she was human, but he was trying to find out if that meant she had limitations, if she was truly vulnerable like a human. She said something like, "I don't fancy dying at the mouth or hands of a Vampire, especially *Blayne*. And the idea of his mouth anywhere near mine makes me shudder. Just him being in my personal space is repulsive." That's what I liked about her. Raven could be funny and she *could* be honest. And it was awesome.

But she couldn't honestly admit her friends were gone. At times she acted like they never existed. Not a flat out delusion, Raven wasn't nuts. She just ignored most conversations on any topic Jet, Ganesha, and Sheba related. This wasn't just in June. It continued on... it lasted for as long as she was...alive. Sometimes, even I have a hard time saying *died*. Dead. Dead. There's that word. Raven's dead. I guess we all have trouble admitting things to ourselves...

I thought my jealousy had ended with punching Olsen and disturbing her club. And that I had left all of that behind in South Carolina. That I could let her be with anyone. But that was before I walked in my uncle's house…

~~~

Chapter 7
King Eben

I'M BEGINNING TO FEEL AS IF I'M suffocating. I push the window up, opening it. It's about ten degrees cooler outside and the breeze calms me down. Thinking about my oldest cousin, Eben, tends to get me all worked up. I stand there for second; just enjoying the cool breeze. I decide that my desk needs to be over here underneath the window. I move it and sit down in the chair and relax. The air feels so good blowing on my face. Right now seems like a perfect time to write.

October 11

Usually Leon's brother isn't around. He's almost a year older than Leon and he goes to college. But for some unknown reason Eben continues to live at uncle's place during the summer. I guess maybe because it's the only home he has and doesn't want to face what he did.

I don't feel bad for him. He brought it upon himself.

Eben also doesn't tell anyone when he plans on being around; he doesn't bother with things like courtesy and consideration.

*(Back in June.
Right after we got back from SC.)*

"So this is the one who saved the world? Joe you didn't tell me she was sexy hot," Eben gleamed lustfully at Raven and tried fixing his dumb, short brown hair.

This is what I was forced to deal with when I walked in my uncle's living room.

"You told him? About her?" I asked Uncle Joe. He was sitting in his recliner reading the newspaper. "You told Mr. King of Whores—complete womanizer here, about <u>her</u>?"

"He was eventually going to run into her. What did you think was gonna happen, son?" He looked up from his paper. <u>"She lives in your house!"</u> I knew he had a point, but still...

My charming cousin stood up from where he was sitting, on the couch next to Rachel, and introduced himself to Ray. "Hi. I'm Eben. The Whore King," he shook her hand.

"So do you want to seduce me now or later?" Raven asked, grinning in my direction, trying to get a rise out of me. I knew my eyes were bulging, about to pop out and land on the floor away from my jealous brain. "That's not funny," I said.

Rachel certainly thought differently. "Yeah it kinda is dude," she said laughing from the couch. "Want to know how to keep your cousins away from your friends? Shoot him with a BB gun," she loudly whispered at me from across the room. And I remembered that one time when she shot me with a BB gun for having sex with one of her older friends.

"Whoa." Uncle Joe quickly stopped reading his newspaper and looked at all of us through his reading glasses. "There will be no more shootings on my property," he told us so sternly that those of us related to him had to refrain from laughing.

Then out of nowhere Eben decided to confess everything. "When I was younger, I burned down me and Leon's house—our parents' house after they died and the three of us came to live with our uncle. I also set his parents' place on fire," he pointed at me. "We'll that sums it up. There you have it," he told Raven.

"How can you say it like that? So causally? Without any remorse?" Leon demanded.

"It's been years, Leon. I think it's time you and Princess Buttercup got over it," he called me before walking out of the living room. Later that night I came back after my Uncle had left and I stormed into my dear cousin's bedroom and delivered a message. He was sitting in his chair playing Xbox and wasn't quick enough to move. I punched him right in the face! It was the first time since the first time I beat him up for burning down our childhood homes.

"Princess Buttercup says to stay away from Raven."

I spent the rest of the summer doing my best to make sure Eben stayed away from Ray. It didn't seem right to keep tabs on Raven so I didn't. I knew Eben had a way of getting to girls and women through text messages. He was after all the King. I wasn't going to go through Ray's phone, but me and Leon didn't have a problem with going through Eben's. Being the genius that he is, Leon easily accessed his brother's phone records to make sure his brother took my threat seriously. I didn't want them speaking to each other. I didn't even want them in the same room. Leon made sure he wasn't sending her texts or calling her and Rachel helped us by telling us whenever he left the house so that made it easier to avoid him.

Rachel kind of felt bad about what she was doing—keeping tabs on her cousin. Her relationship with Eben was nothing like me and Leon's; they are civil to each other. But Rachel knew that Raven dating Eben wouldn't be the best thing for her. And despite Loki's former attempts, Rachel ended up liking Ray. It wasn't until my birthday but they ended up becoming friends. I never knew Loki was the reason for Rachel being borderline rude to Raven when she first came here until I read Ray's diary the other day.

Before July, there was this one time in June, the only time I couldn't keep them away. Leon's birthday. Eben showed up after being M.I.A for a week. And Lana and Cricket came back for Leon's birthday. Leon wanted to have them here. The Shadows had spent a lot of time together. I don't know what they did during that time. I assumed they hunted Vampires. And couple stuff since they were obviously dating now; holding hands and kissing every now and then.

Leon and Rachel walk through the grass, distracting me from my writing. I look out the window to see what they're doing. They set down arm loads of headstones. Apparently Leon really is going all out this year. I suddenly recall Rachel calling me earlier and I ignored her. I bet the reason she called was to give me the heads up on more of this Halloween taken over. I get the feeling she knows that it bothers me but that I won't saying anything to Leon. He has every right to do this.

Brighton and I are so different. He wanted to go to KY kingdom and ride rollercoasters for his birthday. And for my mine I wanted a different kind of ride...

We loaded the car early in the morning for the trip to Kentucky. (The car Raven now had. It wasn't as cool as her other one, the one she destroyed in the zombie apocalypse. We took her car because she said we should save the Chevy Biscayne's life span and that her ride had more space. Raven never really drove her car though. She didn't seem to care for vehicles as much anymore. In fact, that was the first time she drove since May 10. I wonder why? Actually I know why now. Driving was probably another reminder of her friends. And she was on the run from anything that reminded her of them. She didn't drive again until September 31. <u>I will never forget that freaking day</u>...)

Well Leon, Rachel, Raven, Cricket, Lana, and I were putting our luggage in the roomy vehicle, we only planned staying the day but we packed in case Leon and Raven started seeing stuff, past and present, when Eben showed up at Uncle Joe's with "friends". Guys and girls. I assumed he was fooling around with one of those college chicks. They ignored all of us. "Today's your brother's birthday," I reminded Eben. "Happy birthday," he said in the most... uncaring Eben way. And they disappeared inside. I just shook my head. "What did you expect, Luke?" Leon asked me. The entire situation hadn't been anything out of the ordinary. It was normal. Eben and his friends paying little attention to those around them.

The ride to Kentucky was normal except that Mozart wasn't with us. Raven left him at Joe's because he obviously couldn't stay inside the vehicle the whole time. It was a little odd not having to put down a blanket to collect all of his fur like we did when we left for South Carolina. But I actually had fun with Raven. And Lana and Cricket and my cousins on the rollercoasters. It was exhilarating.

And it was completely normal. No interruptions to go here or there. Just plain ole' normal human fun I realized that night as I laid awake next to Raven—the first time I volunteered to sleep beside Ray. It was Leon's birthday and he passed out on the couch after we got back that night. He only made it to three beers. Ha ha ha. Oh, I finally got him that copy of poems by T.S. Eliot to replace the one he left at the hotel back in May.

I also learned that night that Shadows can't drink. Or they shouldn't. Or take any drug that clouds the mind such as alcohol, weed, meth, cocaine, heroin, shrooms. Their powers are affected differently according to the drugs taken. Nothing good comes from them being drug induced. It all seemed very...sucky. (The beer and weed part). I don't even want to know what a Shadow would see on hallucinogens.

I guess Raven was wiped out too because she immediately fell asleep after her one beer and a jay. Rachel left immediately after getting here to go out with her best friend Emily. They have been going to the same church since they were born and have kept in touch during Rachel's time off from school. Rach started her freshman year of college this Aug.

This brings me back to Leon's twenty-third birthday.

I told Cricket I would take Raven to my room. He took Raven's bed and Lana slept at Uncle Joe's. We had decided that having a Shadow in each house was safer than two in one. I can't remember when Lana started that, or if it was hers or Cricket's idea, but no one argued.

So on this particular day—June 13—my heart dropped when I saw Eben that morning as we got ready to leave. But that night as Raven slept on my chest it dropped even a little more when I realized the normalcy of the day. And then I knew

HOME

Raven wasn't grieving properly because nothing about her situation was normal. Grieving is a normal human thing. Her routine—her life—changed drastically. I also admitted to myself as I lay looking at the stars outside my window that picking her up and taking her to my room, and me letting her roll over and drape her leg across me wasn't normal.

I'm pretty sure this day set me up for future conversations—one in particular—that lead to her death. That's all I remember about June.

—Lucas Kale

I willingly leave the memory of her peaceful face beside me on that June night; lightening bugs faded and the sound of tree frogs croak away with the incoming October breeze. Pun intended. And here I am. Back to October eleventh. The middle of the month. I get up and walk away from the window. I don't want to watch my cousins setting up decorations. I'm back here, staring up at my ceiling fan going around and around. My fan is on and it's cool outside, but I could care less if I got sick. Raven's dead. And that's my fault.

I close my eyes and I cry for the first time since Raven's funeral. My tears are warm on my face and they soothe me to sleep.

~~~

Chapter 8
July

I PARK THE CAR in front of my house. It's thundering and pouring down rain. The rain is cold against my skin as Raven and I dash from the car to my house. The air conditioning is on and it's freezing when we come in the back by entering through the kitchen.

Raven's white tank top is soaked and her black swim suit shows through; I secretly check her out. I tell her I'm going to get her something to change into so she doesn't have to go across the house and get the floor wet. I go to my room and get her one of my shirts and when I return a small puddle has collected on the hardwood floor. I plan on hanging out with Raven, but when I look up from the puddle... Her flip flops. Her wet legs and shorts. The white shirt clinging to her, easily exposing the dark fabric just barely covering her nipples, and her long blonde hair now wet and crinkled because of the rain makes me change my mind.

I open my eyes, my ceiling fan comes into focus. Was that a dream? No. Just one of the many reminders that life is a string of opportunities and that I had one—the perfect one, and I let it go. I made it go away—in dreamland and in real life; I went to my room and left her.

I realize it's another Fall morning and another day closer to Raven's favorite holiday. This month is never going to end. I want her more than anything. "Raven," I whisper to no one. I desperately want her back. Anything will do; a smell, just something to numb the pain. I scramble up to the safe. I remember that I have Raven's diary and that last night Leon found out and wasn't too pleased. I got up during the night to get a snack. He asked about her diary when I was in the kitchen and I told him the truth. "You've had it this whole time?" He asked, exasperated. Apparently, he had been looking for it right around the time I took it for myself; after he and the others gave me their written thoughts in hopes that sharing their own pain with me would help, and after Uncle Joe gave me my own journal. It was all to convince me to write about my own feelings. And I will never tell a soul about writing about *my feelings*.

But for whatever reason, Brighton said we should use Raven's diary for research. I told him I would let him know if I found anything. That pissed him off even more and I think we had an argument. It was late and I just wanted to urinate and then go back to sleep. I remember him saying, "I put up with a lot of your BS. And you can't just do me this one favor?" He also said something like, "She never belonged to you, Lucas!" I can't exactly remember. But I know I didn't feel too happy about it. I also don't like that I upset my cousin, whom I love like a brother, so much that he grabbed his jacket and his truck keys and took off.

But I just want Raven.

I enter the correct combination and open the safe that I've put in my room. There she is. I quickly open the diary to the next bookmarked page. I pause for a moment—looking at the picture of us from South Carolina. I touch her face and then flip the picture over so I don't have to look at us; kind of like what Ray used to do with Ganesha's, Sheba's, and the Werewolf's pictures after Olsen had them mailed to her from Amsterdam. She only flipped them back upright on her dresser when Cricket was over.

I realize this entry is dated for July but before my dream memory thing of us in the Summer rain. "Good-bye, South Carolina," I whisper and then flip the picture back over so I can see her beautiful oblong face. I lay the red and black diary down on my desk that's now by the window; which I closed after getting up in the middle of the night. I part my plain white and blue curtains; planning on seeing the wide open land but instead I see a massive cemetery with big black and white spider-webs clinging to gravestones. I forgot that Rachel and Leon decorated this side of the yard last night. A part of me wants to slap the curtains back together but I refuse, because I know I'll have to go outside eventually. And since the yard does look pretty cool I decide to face reality. There's nothing I can do. I sit down and start reading; trying to cope with this sad reality.

July 12

I haven't written in a while so where do I begin? I guess the beginning is as good a place as any. Rachel's birthday was on the fourth of July. She invited Lana and me, Emily (her best friend), and two other girls she knew from high school to her camping out birthday party that day/night.

The party started at 5:30 pm. But before Rachel's other friends showed up, Lana unexpectedly showed me The Book. The old, withered book that has my picture in it—the one she used to tell Alec and the others about me when Leon was still The Preventer. She brought it back from her mom's and asked me how my picture ended up in there. I told her Jet thought it would be a good idea for Shadows and Normals to know about me. He was the one that put all those pictures in there. The other ones were of Vampires—the ones not like me, half-human and good. They were bad. And that part about me not being on the side of those monsters had apparently been ripped out; centuries ago I'm guessing. Lana gave me The Book and I said that I should be the one to keep it. I told her thank you before putting it under my sleeping bag in the tent we had set up.

We grilled out. Joe—Rachel's dad—and Kale and Leon did the cooking. When Lucas grilled the hamburgers he told me he was glad Rachel and I are friends. I tried focusing on Rachel but Lucas was just looking so damn hot. His shirt was off because of the heat. He and Leon and Cricket chased us girls around with the hose pipes and water guns. I loved it. Lucas was totally flirting with me. I know I shouldn't have stayed and let him flirt with me but I did. I could tell he was flirting with me because his eyes were a little glossy with booze and he completely ignored the other girls—even Lana & Rach. I could understand not wanting to flirt with Rachel's friends after her shooting him, but not even a squirt in their direction? Really? "Not even a birthday drench for the birthday girl?" (Those were Rachel's words.) So that proves I haven't gone totally insane.

Kale made it clear I was on his mind. I went over to the grill to get a beer off the table—he purposely kept my favorite kind over there next to him. I reached for one of the bottles, twisted the top off, and took a sip. Just then his favorite song started playing, a song by AC/DC, and he closed the lid on the grill. He quickly finished the last of his beer and he suddenly put his arm around my waist. His other hand was in my hand and then we were slow dancing. He twirled me and brought me in close to him. His smooth face was halfway on mine and halfway in my hair. He lingered against me, smelling my hair. We remained this way for an unusual amount of time. His arm cupped around me, me pressed against his chest, his other hand at the base of my head. I can still remember the rhythm of his breathing; it was as if he was trying to make a decision.

I knew people had to be looking at us now, even though I had my eyes closed. They had to be. This wasn't our normal. I didn't know what Luke was going to do. About us. He...he suddenly pulled away from me and left. He took off to the woods. Back to his house I assume. Just when I am positive he doesn't have feelings for me Kale does something like that. For the rest of the day I was left wondering what the heck that was about...?

After Rachel's birthday cookout—we continued to play horseshoe and other games after Kale left. When I went inside a couple of time to use the bathroom, the news was talking about a woman that had recently gone missing from the county over. Megan Shirley. I don't know why this bothered me so much...I guess it freaked me out because she was my age. My new age. Right now it's July 12 and she's still missing...

(I remember this news story. Megan Shirley was found dead on the fourth of August in an old abandoned gas station. She was apparently beaten to death. A month later Caitlin Fowler went missing. Not only was she the same age, but she lived across the street from Megan. Caitlin's the sheriff's daughter and even to this day no one has been able to find her… I shudder away the creepiness and go back to reading.)

Lana told me that she told Loki they couldn't be friends anymore. I don't know the exact details. She didn't volunteer much and no one wanted to press the issue. Rachel obviously hadn't invited Loki. If I know Loki, she probably became possessive of Lana. Didn't like her hanging out with Rachel and me; which is odd considering she didn't seem to mind Lana spending so much time with Cole and now Cricket.

But it seems Loki wanted revenge of some twisted sorts. It was a great birthday slumber celebration—food, movies, a little booze, a little weed—well it was Rach's birthday so she had a little more :)

Loki ruined it all. Well she tried. I woke up during the night covered in <u>worms</u>. Worms. Lots of slimy slithering worms *running their worm bodies all over me—except my private parts. They were on my legs, my thighs, my stomach, and my arms. I almost freaked out. She almost had me. But then I remembered. I calmly rose up as she busted into the tent ready to take pictures. "You forget who I used to be." I reminded her as I stood up, worms falling to the floor; several stayed on me. "More than once I had to sleep in the dirt."*

Rachel's friends were next to me picking the wiggly critters off me. Lana snatched the cell phone out of Loki's hands and before anyone could stop her, Rachel tackled Loki to the floor. She broke one of Loki's teeth before Lana pried Rach off of her. "Rachel, it's okay," I told her. "Get off of my property!" she screamed at Loki. Loki actually started walking away. Willingly.

Rachel's friends immediately started wrapping the worms up with the sheets and sleeping bags. "I guess we're having a fire tonight," Rachel sighed. Just then we heard Lana and Loki shouting outside of the tent. "You thought THAT would make me your friend?" We couldn't hear what Loki said, but Lana turned around and came back inside the tent.

Rachel burnt those sheets that night in the campfire. It was dark and humid and we were a little hungover—except Lana, obviously. Rach said washing the sleeping bag and sheets wouldn't be good enough. That they would always remind her of Loki. And she didn't want anything that had to do with Loki in her house. The sleeping bag burned, lighting up a good portion of the backyard, and Lana tossed the picture she kept with her—the only hard copy of her, Loki, and Cole together—into the flames. And I tossed that big, old book I had stored underneath the sleeping bag earlier. Glad no one asked about it.

We all leaned on each other. Us girls. We leaned on each other for support as we watched the fire. I'll never forget it. It meant so much. For Lana it was officially admitting that her old trio was no more. Cole was dead and this burned the ties between her and Loki. I feel bad for Lana. It really is my fault they aren't friends. Loki acted this way because I existed. Exist. The fire burned down and pushed the darkness away. I slept wonderfully that night.

Lucas later made it clear we are just "really good friends". Fine. Whatever. I still don't know what to do though about other things. I haven't gotten a single Order since that...night.

(I knew which night she was talking about. Zombie May.)

*I know where my Orders came from— God because I was told so. Not by God, but by **Him**. I haven't seen **Him** in a long time. Not since that time in the panic room right after I became human. I don't know what to do about anything. I have no one to talk to.*

(I don't know what any of THAT means. I still haven't a clue who HIM is.)

Cricket and Lana officially moved back to the U.S. yesterday. She is staying at Joe's. Cricket lives here and sleeps on Leon and Kale's couch. But it's just until school starts next month and they will be staying in the dorms. The three of us are starting to go mad it seems; trying to figure out how to get that Demon out of Loki's mom, and find information about that witch the Demon used when he trapped Leon, Lucas, and me in that house when we were in South Carolina.

And without us, probably because she knew how we would react, Lana went to her neighbor's house—Loki's mom's, to see how the woman acted in general and to see if she could find some useful information there. She couldn't find anything. Not even Loki's mom...

I recall all of this; Rachel's birthday party on July fourth, Lana and Cricket moving in on the eleventh, and then I think about the time Raven was standing soaking wet in my dining/kitchen area after we dashed through the rain.

It hadn't really rained all Summer and my uncle's corn was in bad shape. Uncle Joe started irrigating it from the creek but it still didn't help and the creek was nearly dry. After Lana moved back, she said she knew a thing or two about growing corn because that's one of the crops her father used to grow in Nebraska when he was alive. She mixed up some chemicals and ran it through the irrigation system. I wondered why none of us ever heard of them—not even my super genius cousin... Within two days the corn changed drastically. Lana is quite the agronomist. And the third day that Lana was here it actually rained... This was before my dream that actually happened at the end of the month. The climate went back to the way it usually is; hot, but stormed once or twice a week. The corn shot up and ended up being the best in the whole state—not just the county. Lana saved our corn.

Thinking about Lana reminds me of Loki. I wonder why I never heard about her sneaking into the tent and putting worms on Raven? I wish I had known before I...

And now I think about Cricket. What he wrote in his first entry. The word *betrayal* comes to mind. Again. I immediately feel sick to my stomach. I stop staring at the page and look out my bedroom window at the fake skeletons and bats watching over the new cemetery. I get my pen and journal out from the safe; I have decided to keep them in there with the others' private thoughts.

October 11

When Loki broke the sword—before that messed up worm incident, was the last time I had seen her. I didn't see Loki again until September when Ray... and during the funeral in October. A big part of me wishes that had been the last time. On October 8, I went to work and then had another night of Halloween movies with Leon. I also think this was the day someone came and towed our Chevy Biscayne (that Leon and I shared; that had been in our family) to the junkyard. On the ninth, I went to work and came home to an empty house. Leon had been called to work. And that's when Loki came over and came on to me. Since she is eighteen now I let her. We played a video game and drank. Loki was terrible at the game and that's what lead her to flirting with me. Soon she was on my lap with her tongue in my mouth. She wore a skirt so my fingers were—

When we were making-out Cricket's word <u>betrayal</u> rang big in my mind. I could clearly see it written down in his journal as if it were in front of me. Even though Raven is gone I couldn't bring myself to have sex with her enemy. So much to Loki's disappointment I told her to leave. Even *though I stopped it before things went further, I still feel like I betrayed Raven. As if I defiled her memory.*

If Raven were alive...
—**Lucas Kale**

~~~

Chapter 9
What Happened In August

August 5

Since Rachel will be in college and won't be able to help with the crops and animals Raven hired some more workers for my uncle's farm. I pitched in too. I feel bad for not helping out sooner, but my own business just started seeing profits not that long ago. I had to pay back my business loans and whatever profits I made I saved for our road trips; due to my Preventions in the past. But the farm seems to be doing extremely well this year; the corn especially… Next year Uncle Joe could probably pay the workers himself.

When Cricket came to the clinic the other day, I hired him and Lana part-time when they moved here, we talked (hand-written conversation) about Raven. I'm grateful for what she's doing, helping my uncle. But her constantly trying to get rid of the evil (that she obviously feels responsible for since her death made it possible for all this stuff to exist) in the world makes it seem like she's focusing on everyone's problems except her own…We aren't mad at her or anything of that sort. It's just…complicated.

We tried seeing if Ray's nightmares and night terrors were over. She slept by herself last night, but again they returned. Cricket laid down with her to calm her down but that seemed to make things worse. This proves my theory; that Raven's night terrors are more than likely guilt induced. They are over Ganesha, Jet (the Werewolf), and the Shadow (Sheba). I'm positive having Cricket around makes it harder on Raven.

I don't know what to do… Raven refuses to mourn the loss of her friends—family. She's been on the run from her feelings for quite some time now. I've been trying to find a way to talk to her without her shutting down or leaving. I would hate for her to leave… But she is becoming more and more human-like as the months pass. I fear her leaving, but I also fear what will happen if she continues to refuse to grieve, to deal with what happened; face the emptiness, whatever she feels—all of it.

I have a very bad feeling… If Raven doesn't work this out soon, if Luke and I don't properly handle this… I just know something bad is going to happen as a result. Unfortunately, I don't think any of us know how to truly help her. Not even Cricket.

B.L.C

August 15

I've officially started college! I'm happy, but I'm also sighing right now because this leads to Loki, who used to be my best friend. She called me at the beginning of the month, trying to make up. She promised she wouldn't do anything like that to Raven again (cover her with disgusting, slimy worms). I told her that was good, but our friendship officially ended that night after her atrocity. And that I wouldn't be rooming with her in college, and that Rachel and my mother talked me into going here.

"Too bad you're going to college in Nebraska. It would be cool if we were roommates. They haven't given me one yet, so there's still time..." Rachel said. And so that's how I ended up attending school here in the south! The three of us, Rachel, Cricket, and me!!!!!

Loki asked how I could afford out of state tuition and I told her I couldn't. Raven paid for it. (I didn't want her to but she put it in my bank account. That she also got me.) I told her I wished her the best of luck and then I ended the conversation.

And then the weirdest thing happened yesterday, my first day back at school. Loki had supposedly gotten early acceptance into the dorms back there at the end of July, but yesterday she showed up on campus. She told me that her father who lives in Georgia had saved a lot of money for her college and that basically she could go anywhere in the U.S. and she chose to go here...

Said she's trying to show me she's trying to change, to be a better person, and that she just couldn't go to college up there because of her mom. That it's hard with her mother having a Demon in her. And that she's kind of lost everything she knew...

But how can I stay around her after what she has done to Raven? Sadly, I don't think there will ever be an end. It's crazy how you think life is taking you one way but instead takes you in an entirely different direction.

I love Tennessee though! It's so hilly and there are trees everywhere! Rachel makes the best sweet tea. And country fried steak is now my favorite food. I don't know why, but I also like the smell of the tobacco barns being fired up.

—L.Queen

Ps. I stopped dreaming about Cole and his eerie/cryptic message saying to save her... My last dream was over a month ago before Rachel's party. I was right; if I just ignored them and focused on something else the dreams would go away, and getting rid of that picture of us would help. But I had another dream/nightmare last night... I think seeing Loki is the cause of it...

My feet stop rocking and the porch swing stops. I hurl Lana's diary and it skids around on my porch, bending some of the pages. But I don't care. It was either do that or rip down this Halloween crap that's strung up for tomorrow. It's been two and a half weeks since I've picked up their words and read them. I've been at the shop every day that we're open. I haven't prayed, but I've been wishing Leon would get a Prevention, vision—or whatever you call *seeing the past*. I desperately want to get away from this place—*this house!* I honestly don't know how I'm going to survive tomorrow…

College. That's what started this stupid mess as I recall. I walked in one day and overheard Raven in her bedroom having an argument with Olsen when she was on the phone. *"I don't belong there. I have no place there."* But Olsen told her she didn't have a place *here*, and that she belonged there in Amsterdam, going to school.

She had Pretty Boy Olsen on speaker phone, and since they were arguing it made me happy. I turned on the television to let her know someone was around and that I wasn't spying. Not long after, Raven came out of her room and recanted what happened. "He talked about how I should start applying for colleges. I don't know why he wants me to. I stopped listening after something about rules and regulations," Raven said mockingly and stuck out her in tongue in disgust. "Bottom line, he wants me to go to school this Fall. And that's just ridiculous. I never even went to Kindergarten, what the heck do I need college for? I mean I own my own business." She laughed.

Raven made a valid point. But then I started thinking. More and more I began to wonder about what was best for Raven. The next day Pretty Boy Olsen called me when I was in one of these thinking moods. He told me Raven was just using us and hunting down supernatural creatures as an excuse to not come home. "She hasn't seen her friends' rooms, she hasn't even been in her own room! She can't run forever, Lucas. If you care for her what so ever you will send her back here... Her friends are dead—and she is hiding behind you all. You know sending her home is the right thing to do. But we both know you don't do that."

I didn't want to admit it, but he really got me thinking. It all made sense. She didn't want to go to Amsterdam her home or grieve properly. She didn't really want to spend a lot of time with Cricket because she didn't really know how to help him grieve because she wasn't grieving herself. She wanted to spend even less time around Olsen. As far as I know she only saw him once since the memorials. And that was at her club in South Carolina back in June. Olsen represented a foreign country—Amsterdam, mansion, and the living quarters of her ex-friends.

She didn't want to lament the deaths of her friends. Instead, Ray wanted to spend her human minutes, days, and months, slaying Vampires, sending poltergeist on their way, and trying to figure out how to exorcise a possessed person; chasing false leads one after another.

Most humans tend to go to college and Raven didn't want to do anything that was normal. That was…human.

I don't know why this made me mad, but I threw my phone against the wall. That's a lie. I know exactly why I was mad. Olsen knew something was wrong with her before I did. Even though back in June I confronted her about not shedding a single tear, I gave up… I gave up trying to help her, but Olsen didn't. It wasn't until then when I thought about Leon's birthday, Raven and I sleeping in the same bed, and her having to sleep with either Leon or me because nothing or anyone else could stop the night terrors. I knew that wasn't normal but I dismissed it.

I realized I had given up and accepted her presence for my own selfish reasons. And Leon, too. There was no legit reason for why we didn't suggest getting professional help, or why we continued to allow Raven to live with us. We loved her and didn't want her to go; that was the reason. Leon was in love with her, too; even though he never told her or said anything to me about how he felt. But he did tell me he thought she shouldn't be focusing on romantic relationships at all until she could emotionally handle everything that happened in May. As for college, Leon said that was up to her. "He wasn't going to push".

I pushed. Not hard at first. But after Lana and Cricket joined Rachel for their freshman year I pushed.

Guilt booms out of me like a volcano. I yell and then snatch Leon's journal off the swing, yank Lana's up off the porch, and think about smacking that witch that had been placed beside the front door. But I don't. I couldn't destroy what my cousins had worked so hard on. Instead, I shut the door on the furnace burning inside of me and storm to my room. Once inside, I let the heat out. The two journals I hold ricochet off my wall, and I rip through my desk faster than a twister, knocking everything off; pens, knickknacks, and the picture I framed and put there last week. I had remembered taking a picture with my phone of Raven sleeping on my chest after Leon's birthday. I hear the glass crack as it also hits the wall.

I can't do it… I'm not ready…

I haul ass through my house, leaving Lana's diary and taking mine and Leon's journals. I fling open the front door and tear off to the woods. It's late in the afternoon and I can see my breath so I know it must be chilly. But inside I'm burning up. I sit down on a fallen tree limb and prop up against the tree trunk the limb fell in front of; the leaves have completely fallen off and the bare bark strangely soothes me.

It's October 30. I think and think. Tomorrow's Halloween. How can I possibly face what I've done?

Chapter 10
Raven's Thunder

(The past)
September 30

RAVEN HUNG UP ON Olsen for the third time that week. She knew he meant well, but nothing he proposed seemed like reasons to go to school. It was over a month ago that Cricket started college with Lana and Rachel, and Olsen kept saying, "It would be good for you", and some other stuff Raven tuned out. She opened the door to her bedroom—the one at Kale and Carmany's—and plopped down on the bed. She was mad at Olsen and she scrolled through her phone looking for someone to vent to. Raven realized she no longer talked to most of the people she knew. And she felt like she couldn't talk to Rachel, Lana, or Cricket about this, or much about her life really—not even Cricket knew about Him; the bluish being with wings that used to communicate with her frequently.

Her eyes started to moisten, Raven knew she was about to cry and she quickly dropped the phone on the bed and ran to the kitchen. She needed to find something to clean. There weren't many dirty dishes but she decided to go ahead and get them out of the way. The TV was on in the living room and she saw Caitlin Fowler's photo again; the sheriff's daughter was still missing and now there was a one-hundred thousand dollar reward for anyone who knew about her whereabouts.

Raven finished hand washing the dishes, even though there weren't that many and she could have just put them in the dishwasher. She tended to clean a lot. She did anything to keep busy. Even cook when she wasn't hungry; fixing cookies and brownies for others so she could purposely clean the mess. Raven hated down time—being by herself. She didn't know what she would do without her dog. Mozart was truly her best friend.

After cleaning, the two of them went outside and she tossed his ball around. Raven played fetch with her gray and white Siberian Husky. She even rolled around in the grass with him, and he let out a few excited howls when Leon pulled up in his truck. He was back from an emergency visit at one of his clinics. Kale was only a few seconds behind him; done with work for the day.

The three of them changed clothes and climbed in the car after putting down a blanket to catch Mozart's fur. Leon was excited about Halloween shopping. Raven even had Lucas excited; even though he tried so hard not to show his enthusiasm it was obvious. After arriving at the Halloween store they walked up and down the aisles looking at the creative displays; masks with fake blood and fur, wigs in all colors, moving and talking witches and skeletons. They had a variety of costumes and Raven kept her options open.

A French-maid costume! Dear god I can barely control myself right now with her just wearing a skirt, Lucas thought and looked away from the sexy outfits. He tried his best not to look at Raven's bare legs, but she was walking directly in front of him and she looked beautiful in the red skirt and white top.

I wonder if the two of us could do a theme? I'll mention it later, thought Leon while he continued pushing the cart down the aisle.

Surveying the merchandise, they came up with ideas for later, but for now they got a few items for inside the house; a cool looking fake book of spells that had a skull of top, some wall decorations, orange and black pumpkin streamers, and a few other things. They put the stuff in the trunk and then walked Mozart around in the grassy area outside before taking off to pick up food from the *Olive Garden* for dinner.

When they got back to the house Leon was tired from working at the clinic so he called it a day and went to bed early. Lucas decided it was time. He tossed a college brochure on the coffee table.

"I'm not going," she flat out told him.

"Why?"

"Because there are more important things to do. You know this."

"Why can't you see the *present* while you're at college?" Lucas asked. "I have my shop. Leon has his clinics."

"So?"

"Do you even know what makes you happy?"

"Well, right now it's not you. That's for sure."

"Either go to school or grieve the deaths you choose to ignore." He gave her an ultimatum.

"Excuse me?"

"Or you can't stay here anymore."

"What?" Raven's voice was high-pitched and she was clearly hurt. "I-I-I…"

Lucas could tell she was fighting back tears. But then she suddenly became angry. Raven snatched her purse off the counter. The screen door slammed loudly behind Raven and Mozart as she stormed out of his house. She got Mozart inside her car and was about to open the driver door when Lucas blocked her with his arm. "Don't do this, Ray." "You already did," she said and pushed his arm out of the way.

"If you get in that car don't come back."

Raven glared at him and started the engine. She sped down the gravel driveway and hightailed it out onto the road. Lucas watched her lights until she finally disappeared out of sight. Lucas Kale couldn't believe what just happened. He went back inside and sat down at the kitchen table and rubbed his face ruefully. *Was she really gone?*

He waited several minutes and then picked up the phone and called Olsen. Lucas had a feeling that's whom she would turn to even though he, too, wanted a better life for her just as much as Lucas did. "Where is she going, Olsen? *Shanghai?*" Lucas nearly dropped the phone.

"Picture a pissed off teenager. Now picture a recently turned teenager with unlimited resources at their disposal. I don't know what you said, but at least she's closer to being home," said Olsen.

Lucas hung up, and then dialed Raven. Surprisingly, she answered. "This is why I can't date you." He needed to say something to grab her attention and Lucas knew that would do it. "Shanghai? *Really,* Raven? Just leaving and flying far away from me just because you know I'm right? Running from your problems. Don't you think that's a little immature?"

"I'm nineteen, and I've only been a teenager for a few months, Lucas. What's your excuse?"

"Raven."

"You're never going to love me, Lucas."

"You're wrong. Actually I love you very much and want you to come back… Please come back so we can talk."

Raven hung up. She was completely shocked and caught off guard. Her mind was racing. She shifted the gears so she could accelerate faster to pass the tractor slowly moving along on the road. It was night time but it wasn't uncommon to see farming equipment being used and moved around between farms this time of the year here.

Raven's phone rang again and she answered with her Bluetooth. Olsen told her his private jet was ready and she take it. She knew he was in Nashville on business and would book a flight soon to meet up with her in Shanghai.

"I can't wait to see you," Olsen told her.

"I can't wait to see you, too." Raven said and hung up. She passed a sign pointing the way to the interstate for Nashville. She down shifted and made a U-turn. What was she thinking? She couldn't leave. Not like this. She was trying to get her thoughts together; to figure out what she was going to do. Raven didn't know what she was going to say, but she knew she had to go back to Kale and Carmany's.

A vehicle went around the tractor she had passed on the two-way road. The vehicle had plenty of time and room to get back over, but for some reason it stayed in her lane… The vehicle wasn't showing any signs of getting back over and Raven began to panic when Mozart barked from her backseat. The headlights came closer and closer and Raven's heart began to beat faster. She had no choice but to get in the other lane…

Even though she was driving in the wrong lane, Raven thought it was going to be okay. But then the vehicle rammed her in the side. There wasn't a guard rail and Raven slid down the side of the embankment. She prayed the creek wasn't deep enough to drown them…

After the car landed on four wheels, Mozart jumped upfront to check on his master. He licked the blood dripping from her forehead… What was wrong with her?

* * *

Lucas was sitting in the living room when Loki called, reading a book Raven had suggested a few days earlier. He was confused as to why the young girl was calling and at this hour of the night. "You need to get here. It's Raven," she said and gave him her current location.

Lucas flew into Leon's bedroom and told him to get dressed. "Lucas, what?" Leon looked horror-stricken as he put his pants on.

"We gotta' go. It's Ray. I don't know what, but something has happened to her." Lucas hurried out of the bedroom and to the truck.

"Whatever's happened she'll be okay," Leon said, putting his shirt on inside Lucas's truck. The rocks from the graveled driveway made tinking noises when the two of them shot out like a bat out of hell.

On the way to Henry's farm, that was closest to the interstate, it seemed to Lucas that Leon had a dozen questions. He wanted to know where Raven had taken off to and why she left. Lucas lied and told him he didn't know where she was going or her reason for leaving.

Finding the scene of the accident wasn't difficult. The flashing emergency lights took over the night like a wild country party in the middle of a cornfield. Henry's property was filled with three police cars, a firetruck, a wrecker truck, and Loki's car. Lucas parked on the side of the road that hadn't been blocked off, and they witnessed Raven's car being lifted from the creek. Loki met them as they crossed the road. "The ambulance just left with her."

"Lucas?" A police officer said with surprise and sorrow in his voice when he approached them. Lucas instantly recognized the cop. He was Brad's brother; his mechanic. "What happened, Clark?"

"I'm sorry, Lucas. I think you should get to the hospital."

Lucas pulled him aside. "What happened?"

"I'm not sure. Her car was obviously rammed in the side. It looks like someone forced her off the road. Possibly a drunk driver."

There was a certain look in his eye and Lucas sensed there was more. "She's dead, isn't she?"

"I'm not a doctor so I have no right telling you this... They've been doing CPR since the blonde chick arrived, but I'm pretty sure Raven was DOA."

"Dead on arrival."

A howl kept Lucas from losing his mind for the present time. A green and blue-eyed dog stood at the edge of the drop off. He happily ran up to Leon.

"He's been down there the whole time," the officer told him. "He ran off whenever someone came near him."

"We'll take him." Lucas nodded and signaled Leon. Mozart trailed close to the veterinarian as the two young men sprinted back to the truck. Lucas started the engine while Leon let the tailgate down for the dog so he could hop in the back.

Loki and the Hunters were the first ones to the emergency room. Lana and Cricket arrived at the hospital just before Olsen. And since Olsen was Raven's emergency contact, the Doctors wouldn't release any information. Lucas didn't tell the others what he was told at the farm. It was the first time he

prayed to God, and he prayed Clark was wrong and that Raven would survive…
* * *

Present

The wind blows and I hear something other than the wind rustling the leaves around in the woods. I highly doubt it's a Vampire since the sun is still out so I ignore it. I can't believe I told Raven not to come back. What was I thinking? I pull the pen out from my pants pocket. Being in the woods by myself seems to make the words flow.

Chronological order:

The night of Sept 31

After finding out Raven died from severe head trauma, we all went back to my uncle's, including Loki and Olsen. I forgot Loki was there. I don't remember much from that night. I remember Olsen tried taking Raven's dog but Mozart acted like he didn't want to leave... It was strange. He growled at Olsen and then whined and then ran away from the house and into the woods... I could tell Olsen was hurt by the behavior, but he asked if he could leave Mozart for the time-being and Leon gladly said yes. Olsen told us the funeral would be here. In TN. That Ray must have changed her will without telling anyone. Apparently she didn't want to be buried in Amsterdam anymore. I don't remember much because Leon, Uncle Joe, and I started drinking. I don't think Uncle Joe drank much but I know Leon and I did.

October 1

About sunrise. Leon and I woke up together on the couch. Our own couch. I woke up and for a split second forgot what happened. But then the pit in my heart punched my soul and it felt as if I had shattered all over. What made it worse was when I went to get some orange juice to kill my super hangover and I saw the Halloween decorations on the kitchen table. The emptiness...darkness inside me thrived all over. I went straight to my room and didn't surface until that night.

When I woke up and went back to the kitchen, only because I was starving, Leon had already put out several of the decorations he and Raven picked out at the store. I got the juice that I was originally going to get and made a sandwich. Afterwards I tried putting the decorations away but somehow it just felt wrong. And I didn't really have the energy to fight with my cousin so I just let it be. I took a shower and bailed. I ended up at a bar and I had sex with a bleach blonde. Her hair was long and she reminded me of Raven.

October 2

I came back to my house. I was already in a bad mood and seeing what little decorations there were in the house made it worse. I guess I blamed the end table in the living room for not curing me because I made it pay. Luckily I was the one who bought it so Leon didn't have to get another one.

October 3

I woke up beside a natural blonde that morning. Her hair was shorter, but I liked that it was real. I drove back to my house in the Biscayne. I looked in my mirror. I felt nothing. I crawled back in my bed and I didn't come out of my room until the next day. Not even to eat.

October 4

This was basically some sort of intervention. After the delivery man dropped off the white roses I ordered for Raven's funeral, my cousin and the others gave me their journals, Lana her diary. A sort of "We all have pain" "Learn to deal in a healthy way". And "here's something to distract you." That was after lunchtime. I said thanks, but I didn't tell them I wasn't intending on reading so much as a word. I felt nothing. I felt numb. I didn't think about anything. I didn't plan on doing anything. I sat in my room staring at the walls. It was about sunset when I finally decided to get some fresh air. I went outside and sat in the car.

It was as if there was nothing in the world to care about. She was gone and I had nothing. I felt like I had been the one who had died. But I wasn't dead. And that was a problem because I wished I was. I almost wished I could make a deal with God. Take me instead of her. I would wish Raven alive even if it meant I, myself, would pass away. If Raven got to live I would feel something. Something other than this—this nothing. This empty, blank space that seemed to run as deep as the Earth is wide.

HOME

I sat behind the wheel of the car staring out straight ahead at the field before me. But I didn't really see anything outside of myself. I remembered all the times she was in my car. "I love you," I said out loud. Then I finally felt something. A spark. Just a spark. But it was enough to motivate me. I took out my pocket knife and shredded it. The front seat. I shredded it like it was paper. When I was done I opened the door and the spark ignited in me again and I broke into full speed towards the house. I picked up my baseball bat from my room and before I knew it I was back out on the lawn with the bat at my side. I gripped the handle and swung the bat back. The blow dented the trunk. Once. Twice. Three times. It wasn't enough. I moved to the back windshield and hit it until it shattered. The spark in me was rising and rising. I smacked the bat up against a passenger window and it gave in easier than the back windshield did.

The tears come and instead of putting out the spark inside of me they acted as fuel. "Ahhhh!" I screamed in rage, swinging the bat backwards and forwards until I took out the rest of the windows. The loud sound of breaking glass was still no match for the painful thunder seizing my heart. By this time my spark had grown into something else. I ran to the basement and got the gas and a lighter. I got in the car, whipped it in reverse, and moved it further away from the house. Leon came running out, hair wet, apparently he had been in the shower. I poured the gasoline on our Chevy Biscayne and then Leon tried to stop me from what I was about to do. But I pushed him down and I set it on fire. I couldn't control the flow of my tears anymore than I could control Raven's death. It burned and burned. Leon finally managed to drag out the hosepipe and put the flames out.

I got in bed that night thinking about the streams of anger that had escaped down my face. It felt like rain on a hot summer night.

October 5

But then morning came and I realized it wasn't summer anymore and Raven was just as dead as the falling leaves outside my window. And her funeral was in a few hours. I ate breakfast and then I looked at myself in the bathroom mirror. I thought about the two women I slept with after finding out Ray died. I slept with those women just to replace Raven. I punched the bathroom mirror so hard it broke and I cut my hand. It wasn't anger I felt. Not like last night. For the first time in my life I felt disgusting. Several drops of my blood landed on the white rose petals I had put on the counter for Ray's service.

After I got cleaned up and dressed, I grabbed the flowers and we all left. The funeral is kind of a blur now. I remember there was a bunch of people I didn't know. And I know I saw Lana comforting Cricket. It actually hurt to see him in that much pain. I hate seeing Cricket cry. He didn't cry at the hospital, but Olsen did. I don't think I ever realized how close Olsen and Raven were until that day.

I remember what Rachel said to Loki. "I guess now that Raven's gone you get my cousin all to yourself." "You're right," Loki said. "I didn't like her. But I'm not a monster. I would never wish this."

I know that it rained. Not much though. It was weird. The sun kept trying to come out. At one point—after Raven's casket was lowered into the dirt and I tossed my roses on top, they still had my dried blood on the white petals—the sun was out while it was still raining.

After her funeral I found myself sitting outside on the back porch drinking a beer. "I see what you did to the car," my uncle said coming around the house.

"What about it?"

"Did it help?"

"Not for long." I took a drink. A big drink.

"Didn't think so."

A notebook and pen landed in my lap. "What is this, Joseph?"

"A virgin stripper." He sat down beside me. "What does it look like, boy?"

"I know where this is headed and I'm not going there." I told him and handed the notebook back to him. Uncle Joe pushed my hand away. "She's gone, son. And you have to get it out. But if you keep tearin'

your stuff up you're gonna run out of crap real quick and then, well, you sure as hell ain't coming to my house."

I chuckled.

"There you go," Uncle Joe patted me on the back. "Look. I know what you are thinking. That having a journal is lame or isn't very manly. But if writing on a piece of paper to keep from killing the four kids you are raising and from setting fire to the place you work at isn't manly, then put me in a poke-a-dotted dress and call me Josephina."

The sun is starting to disappear behind the clouds, and sitting out in the woods all by myself is getting freaky. From the look of Leon's journal there is only one entry left. I decide to hurry up and read it. When I finish I am surprised. He talked about these weird dreams he had of Raven after she died. He specifically talked about this reoccurring one where

Raven appeared in his bedroom at night like she was a ghost or something. The song *Sweet Dreams* by Marilyn Manson played but it was kind of faded like background noise. And Raven begged him to help her… It was the weirdest thing…

Since that concludes Leon's thoughts and I've read everything there is to read from the others', I think for a moment, and then I close the damn thing. It's been a month since I saw Raven. Since I saw her beautiful smile. I jump from the log and dash out of the woods and through the maze of decorations. I open the back door to my house and toss the journals on the dining table. I abandon all reasoning and go back down the steps and through the Halloween maze around to the front of my house.

By and by gravel crunches underneath my shoes. I notice the sun has almost disappeared as I come running upon the mailbox. But I don't care that I'm only wearing a short sleeve shirt. It's getting colder out here, but that means nothing to me. And soon my house is far behind me. I run so hard vomit comes up. After stopping, I finally take notice of where I am. I've run the two miles to my nearest neighbor; in the opposite direction of my uncle's. Wally's grim reaper decorations haunting the night send me back into panic mode.

Tomorrow is Halloween—her favorite holiday.

And instead of celebrating, Ray lays in a casket six feet under, I remorsefully think. I can't bare it… It's too much for me. I pushed. I pushed Raven to her grave. I miss her so much. I know what I have to do… There is no way I can survive tomorrow.

STATEN

I've done the research. I have to do this…

~~~~

Chapter 11
October

CAITLIN FOWLER USUALLY woke up the same way she had for...well, she wasn't exactly sure how long she had been in the nasty smelling basement. But something was different. Her wrists were still handcuffed and her feet chained to the bed. But every time she woke up it was morning and no one was ever here that early—it wasn't morning and it was dark. It was nighttime; Caitlin was positive. She glanced up at the bar covered window above her bed. No light. It was still...whatever day it was before she went to sleep.

She had a feeling it was Fall now. Caitlin could see out the window above her bed—the one she was handcuffed to and had been since they grabbed her back in July. The tree outside had lost everything; the leaves turned green and changed color and drifted through the air. Maybe it didn't lose anything; it was still beautiful and still alive. The process hadn't killed the tree—only changed it and prepared it for the next process.

There was an unrecognizable commotion upstairs; Caitlin couldn't make it out but it's what caused her to awake from her medicine induced sleep. Her heartbeat dramatically increased when the light snapped on and footsteps sounded like elephants down the basement stairs. Her kidnappers were in a hurry. Caitlin started to panic; more than the usual panic from being kidnapped. Until now everything happened on a schedule. She couldn't recall how she came to be here, but she was positive drugs were involved. She was the Sheriff's kid and the worst drug she ever did was pot, so it had to be some other kind of drug. The girl had no idea how they did it. Caitlin went to sleep in her own bed and woke up in someone else's basement with three goons standing over her—a blonde, a red head, and a dark haired man.

The dark-haired scraggly guy seemed to be the ring leader. The red-headed boy was really the only one who tried having a conversation with her. He told her he was sixteen and had no family. His blonde friend was nineteen, and the older man was the blonde's stepfather and that he was barely thirty.

For the most part the kidnappers pretty much ignored her. She got fed once a day and switched from the chains on the metal bedframe that was up against the wall to a longer chain located in between her bed and the bathroom located to her right. They kept the conversation to a minimum, just enough comments to keep her spooked.

During her alone time, which was a lot, she thought about her dad. She expected him to come barging in any minute. Each day that he didn't, Caitlin knew the situation was getting worse and worse. She prayed each day for someone to come rescue her. When the sheriff's daughter heard the commotion she had high hopes that at this very moment was her dad's team coming to the rescue.

But then she saw the body.

Caitlin was still groggy and her vision was blurry from whatever sleeping medicine she was given before bedtime. Caitlin squinted. The big man with the scraggly beard gently lowered the body to the ground and propped it against the wall. Caitlin heard chains rattle and locks clicked.

Who's that other person, and what's their plan for us, Caitlin immediately asked herself. *And where's the nicer kid; Red Head?*

The blonde teen looked at Caitlin through his glasses and she became terrified. Then something else happened that wasn't normal. The older teenage boy came at her with a needle and when it pierced her arm Caitlin immediately began to feel like she was floating on clouds. She caught one last glimpse of the body. She was a blonde girl and her head was covered in blood... The sheriff's kid couldn't resist the sandman when he came bearing dreams of home.

* * *

HOME

The missing girl opened her eyes. Caitlin was so lost. Nothing about her surroundings made sense. The ceiling above her didn't ring any bells, and the wall at the foot of the bed and to her left meant nothing to her. This wasn't her house.

Her nose itched and she went to scratch it, but her wrist seemed to be caught in something. Caitlin tugged again, simultaneously trying to move her feet. The weight of the chains reminded her that she was in the basement—someone else's basement. The sunlight blasted around the bars on the window and she thought the light was playing a trick. It had to be a trick… It must be from the sedative; that long ass needle. She clearly remembered when it was stabbed into her veins by the blonde kidnapper. Her eyes must be playing tricks on her. There couldn't be another person…

Caitlin blinked and blinked again, trying to get her eyes to focus. "Someone there?" she asked, and blinked again. Her vision was slowly clearing away the fuzzy stuff.

Then she saw the blonde girl slumped her; her back against the wall.

Caitlin wondered if the girl was even alive. Her eyes finally cleared up and Caitlin saw the calendar; that was also new. It was placed on the far side wall, next to the new girl. The top of the calendar was a picture of pumpkins and at the bottom someone had crossed off October First and Second. Assuming that was correct, today was the Third of October. That's a lot of time to have been asleep.

"Hey! Hey!" the sheriff's daughter whispered. Caitlin tried everything she could; whispering louder and rattling her chains. But the girl never stirred. Something on her forehead caught Caitlin's eye. She stopped moving and focused on the girl. The gnash on her head looked freshly stitched. *Had they patched her up? What the hell is going on...?!* She doubted that she really wanted to know. Nonetheless, she had to use the bathroom. Luckily she didn't have to wait long. Red Head, who was younger than her, came down the stairs about five minutes later with the dark-haired man. Red Head seemed to be the nicest of the three kidnappers but they usually pushed him around; bullied him. He latched the long chain up to her that was hooked in the middle of the room before he removed the chains on her feet. Next he untied her hands while the older man held a pistol at her.

The dark-haired man with a nasty beard handed her a change of clothes and told her to shower after she used the bathroom. Caitlin didn't think that was odd, she only had three showers since she had been here. But then he handed her a razor. She wasn't allowed to shave, and she knew very well why they wouldn't give her a razor. They knew better than to give a cop's daughter any sort of weapon.

Caitlin couldn't remember the last time she ate. She felt weak so she pushed away the questions that were coming to her and peed and then got in the shower. She enjoyed it; the water felt good on her dry skin. When she finished washing her body, Caitlin heard the bathroom door crack open and Red Head told her breakfast was almost ready. Caitlin hurried up and shaved her legs and put on the new clothes and went back out to eat her breakfast. The bacon, eggs, and juice sat on the floor in-between the bathroom and her bed; next to the end of the chain that was hooked to the hard floor. The ginger kid removed the razor from the bathroom, and he and the two of them watched her and the other unconscious female. Caitlin finished eating and went to use the bathroom again; this was the first meal she had eaten in days she only guessed, since right before they brought down the other girl, and her stomach was acting weird.

Caitlin thought about how great the shower was and it made her feel better and she hoped that she and the new girl could form an escape plan. But all hope fled the moment she stepped outside the bathroom door. Caitlin felt something sharp pierce her right arm…

* * *

RAVEN

There was something wet on my head. I felt my dog's tongue lapping over and over across my forehead. And then I felt the wetness turn to ice and the cold burned through me like a forest fire. The ice was so cold I almost expected to wake up in a lake of glaciers.

But then I feel their presence. I don't know how many, but something tells me there's more than one. I open my eyes, and see my legs and red skirt before the water runs from my blonde hair and into my eyes. I open my mouth and let the water in; my tongue and throat feel like needles, and I begin slurping up the wetness. I am still aware that I am not alone, but I don't care. It tastes so good and I'm so thirsty.

"Well, they don't suspect a thing." I hear a young male voice say as his feet bounce down what I believe to be stairs; I have a feeling I'm in a basement. My head starts pounding, or I just realized that it has been throbbing something wicked. I force my eyes open a little wider; milky eyes or not, I don't need clear vision to know I have been taken somewhere against my will. I'm not sure when I felt the chains, heck I don't even know where I'm at or what day it is, but my hazel eyes confirm what I already suspected.

I have no idea, yet, which of my enemies has done this; ran me off the road and who knows what else. I calmly raise my head to face the Vampire or Demon; or possibly Shadow. A light above burns my eyes and my eyelids involuntarily close back together; shying away from the bright piercing light.

"Good, good," a deep, adult male voice says before his lips touch my cheek. I don't know what's more repulsive about the lingering kiss, his breathe or his smelly beard. Booze and chili. This lets me know I'm not dealing with a Vampire. And probably not even a Shadow considering the amount of alcohol I'm smelling.

When he finally pulls away I force my eyes open. He is basically how I pictured him; tall, black beard, and mustache. He wears dark clothing; as do the other two males. One of the guys is a curly blonde wearing glasses and he's a lot younger than the alpha man with the facial hair. There's a teenager with hair similar to a carrot. I've never seen any of them.

What I didn't see in my mind was the look of a criminal standing over his prize. There was no Demon in this man. He was indeed a man—a human; a bad one. I am very much confused. What could these humans possibly want with me?

I groggily stare at the bearded man. I don't know for how long; kind of seems like forever—forever waiting for it to make sense. I fully open my eyes as I lay back against the wall. I'm one-hundred percent conscious this time. My clothes are still wet and I'm cold so I couldn't have passed out for that long. I see that I am chained to a wall; hands and feet. The concrete floor is cold and hard. The blonde teen standing across me from holds a pistol. Weasel, my nickname for the redhead ginger, awkwardly stands by the stairs like an uncomfortable little kidnapping weasel.

There is a calendar on the yellowish wall to my right; according to the days marked off it's the Fifth of October. I look to the left to see what is making one of my kidnappers so uncomfortable. There's a window with bars; no light from the other side. It must be nighttime. There's a bed below the window and a girl is chained to the frame. The girl looks awfully familiar. Where have I seen her? That fluffy brown hair and crooked nose...

I'm not feeling one-hundred percent well and my vision begins to fade again. I think I see the dark-haired man bend down and kiss the girl. I blink, trying to blink my vision back into focus. "Did you hear the good news?" He asks me. I, of course, don't have a clue what he is talking about, I've been unconscious and definitely not watching and listening to any news. "Your funeral was today," he tells me like it's a fact. "But don't worry. Gonna make you feel real good as soon as I'm done here." He starts to loosen what I assume to be his belt. The grogginess is returning. Glasses, my name for the blonde, takes a small step towards me, cautious. *As he should be,* I tell myself.

My vision comes back together—like a drunk mans. The blonde kid, he's probably my age, my human age. I think he puts a white rose in this small clear refrigerator... After he closes the door blondie takes off his glasses and then suddenly grows long blond hair, his eyes turn hazel, and his muscles become feminine. His shirt turns into a white blouse and his pants become a red skirt. I may be all wonky, but I know myself when I see me. The stitches on her forehead probably even look exactly like mine.

The girl with the crooked nose screamed. I can only assume it was from the shock of seeing someone shapeshift. I was just as surprised as she was; only I wasn't about to show it. I had seen Shapeshifters back before The Banish. I just couldn't understand what they wanted with us—with me.

The blonde teen, who now looks like me, presses play on the radio to my right. The dark-haired man climbs on top of the girl. She screams and tries to fight back while the music plays. I know what he is going to do and there is nothing I can do. The beat to *Sweet Dreams* by Marilyn Manson slowly drifts out of the radio, and I close my eyes and go to a world where I dance with Leon and Lucas.

* * *

My eyes snap open. Lucas is gone. Leon is gone. My nice dreams are gone. I roll over from my pile of blankets mounted up on the concrete floor. I immediately look at the Fall calendar.

The calendar says today is October Fifteenth. I'm immediately concerned.

I've been here about two weeks and have yet to see signs of a rescue mission. Heck, I haven't seen much of anything. *Did they touch me like they touched her,* the thought quickly repulses me. But then the disgust and fear subside; I remember that humiliating 'virgin candle' incidence back in July when Lucas, Leon, and me were in South Carolina. I'm a virgin and I don't feel any different. Then again that doesn't mean anything if I was drugged. *But they would want me to be awake for that,* I think—I know, putting myself in the mind of a savage.

I don't remember much during these past couple of weeks. They've kept me heavily sedated; but I do recall them telling me that Lucas and Leon weren't looking for me. I hope that's not true. I miss them so much. I miss my dog.

What's the flower for? One of those crazies brought it down here and put it in a clear freezer. To remind me I'm dead I guess. The rose appears to have red spots on it.

I'm lost.

I have no idea how to save us; the sheriff's daughter and me.

"You're Caitlin right? The sheriff's daughter?" I ask her as she wakes up; I can tell it's morning by the light coming in above her bed. She looks surprised I spoke. I guess she figured I was dead...or never going to join the living.

"You know who I am?" the sickly-looking girl asks, still surprised; then a wave of hope shadows over her boney face. It didn't always look like that; being held prisoner for months with little food would make anyone look like death.

I tell Caitlin her face has aired on every news station nearly every day and featured on every single newspaper since they took her, and that her dad is offering a huge reward.

Caitlin told me she had screamed and screamed for hours and nothing happened. They had to be in a secluded area. We talked about how they treated her; almost decent, let her color and watch movies, until I was kidnapped. She told me they hadn't really touched me; just watched me and gave me meds, and fed me through tubes. The girl told me he did indeed rape her that first night they brought me here. But they paid her little attention since then; fed her every now and then, and occasionally let her use the toilet; which had no window. I vaguely remembered them letting, or having Caitlin help me use the bathroom.

I suddenly feel like I can help. Soothe her. "Do you believe in God?" I ask.

"I did. Before this," she admits.

"Prior to being raped, did you believe good people went to Heaven and bad people went to Hell?"

"I did. Yeah." She cleared her throat. I don't know if it's because she hadn't drank any water in a while or because the subject was difficult.

"Are you a good person?"

"Yes."

"Repeat after me. Psalm 143," I tell her, "Verses 1-4: *'Lord, hear my prayer. In Your faithfulness listen to my plea, and in Your righteousness answer me. Do not bring Your servant into judgment, for no one alive is righteous in Your sight'—*"

The other teen girl not only repeats the verses after me, but she takes over the Davidic psalm. *"'For the enemy has pursued me, crushing me to the ground, making me live in darkness like those long dead. My spirit is weak within me; my heart is overcome with dismay."*

"Verse 7," I begin. *"'Answer me quickly, Lord; my spirit fails. Don't hide Your face from me, or I will be like those going down to the Pit.'"* I swear I see Him—not God, but *Him*; the one I've been seeing for nearly all my life. The one who helped me with my Orders. For a split second I see him— his blue body, his wings hovering behind him, and his dark blue tongue flickers out before he disappears; it's the first time I've seen Him since May. And at first I think I'm hallucinating, but then I know I'm not crazy. It felt too real.

"Verse 8," Caitlin continues; not seeing him. *"'Let me experience Your faithful love in the morning, for I trust in You. Reveal to me the way I should go, because I long for You.'"*

Glasses—the curly blonde, excitedly enters the basement; walking down the steps with a certain bounce. He winks at me and turns on the CD player and *Sweet Dreams* drifts through the basement. He walks past me and over to the other teen girl and tells Caitlin it's his turn this time. I guess he expected Caitlin to yell, or for me to say something when he gets on top of her; naked. But we aren't playing his game. The music playing isn't as loud as before, and I hear her say, "I forgive you. All of you."

I can't exactly see his face, but the boy jerks back and I know he's confused. Then Caitlin's eyes roll back in her head and her body starts shaking. She's having a seizure. The boy jumps off of her, and during the seizure Caitlin hits her head against the bed rail and then her body collapses. Even before he figures it out, I already know she's dead. The boy freaks out and points at me. "You! You did this," he shouts. "What did you do?!" I feel his hand smack my face and then pain at the back of my head when it hits the hard basement wall...

* * *

HOME

October 30

LUCAS

I have to do this... It's a long shot. But it's a shot and I have to take it...

I've run about half a mile from my house towards my uncle's when I meet my neighbor driving from that direction. Wally stops his truck and asks where I'm headed. I tell him the cemetery, and nod in the direction he just came from. He asks me if I want a ride and I say sure. He knows which one I'm taking about. The nearest one; right before you get to the city. Wally turns around on our dirt road, and soon we pass by Uncle Joe's house. I'm quiet and my neighbor doesn't say much or asks me why I've been running. I'm headed to the cemetery; he probably figures someone died, naturally, and doesn't want to pry.

Wally pulls into the cemetery and asks if he should wait and I tell him I'm good; I'd rather walk back to my house. After he leaves, I punch in the security code to the gate surrounding Raven's grave; Olsen set it up and only gave it to a few people; those of us who knew the real Raven, the one who fed on Vampires, and saved us and the rest of the planet from flesh eating cannibals.

This is the first time I have been here since we buried Raven; nearly a month ago. My heart skips a beat when I see her headstone; all alone near the weeping-willow tree. There are fresh flowers on her grave. There's a note that says, ***"I love you. Love, Cricket."***

I immediately feel worse. I sometimes forget Cricket knew Raven longer than I did, and he knew her just as well as Olsen. I don't know what it is about Cricket's grief that just makes it harder for me; like a knife to the kidney. I haven't seen him, Lana, or my cousin since they got back home yesterday for Fall Break.

I can't control it; the tears. They come and I let them. I was in love with Raven, and I basically avoided her half the time and the other half was spent flirting and coming on to her like an immature idiot. Someone ran her off the road and I have no one to beat up; to make pay for the happiness they ripped from me. I sit in front of the headstone and my tears feel cold as the fall wind blows.

Suddenly, yellow, red, and brown leaves fly up around me as Blayne jumps down on the other side of her grave; the fence doesn't keep away creatures of the night. I now realize the sun—God's star—that keeps away the Vampires, has vanished.

That knuckled-headed shell of a teenager has put blonde streaks through his light brown hair. "Could you look more desperate to fit? Miss your Vampire daddy?" The kid just stands there holding a book. The security light reveals me to that it's *Grimm's Complete Fairy Tales*. "So who's the new leader of you morons?"

The teenage vamp opens the book and quotes a passage; something about a cock—a rooster—digging a grave for a dead hen. *Death of the Hen.* It was all ironic and it made me want to kill him. "Are you responsible for her death?" I demand the truth from him.

Blayne smiles. "If I was, you'd be the first I'd brag to. It's not like you're much of a Hunter anymore, right?" He closes the book and turns his back to me; walking on the opposite side of the tree. The brat doesn't know who he's dealing with; he thinks he can just taunt me and smirk away through the night. I just smile and wait. The little jerk gets caught up in the net Leon designed, sending the pile of dead leaves flying through the air, and I move in to give him a permanent kind of darkness.

We had the idea to set up a trap just in case the Vampires or Shadows showed up; they might be the one—or ones—responsible for killing Raven. The code was to keep regular people—even funeral management so that no one would be caught in the traps. So far no one was caught; until now.

I go to stake him. But I'm suddenly stopped by another Vampire. I recognize the bald Vampire from working with Kronos, the Japanese girl, and Blayne and the other bloodsuckers when I was in Kansas. He is dressed in a cape similar to the one Kronos wore before Raven and Lana killed him...

He takes the stake from me and throws me to the gate. I land so hard the wind gets knocked out of me and I stop breathing. I can't move. I can only watch as he frees Blayne. When he finishes cutting the ropes my breathing finally resumes, but I'm almost certain they're about to kill me.

But then the older vamp pushes Blayne and the kid screams that an arrow just barely missed his heart. I see the arrow sticking out of his chest just as the bald Vampire snaps an arrow in half before it touches his torso. I get to my feet and realize my rescuers are a dark-skinned male and a raven-haired girl. But just as the Shadows show up so do other bloodsuckers. Cricket and Lana fight with two vamps and I stake a third one who has his back to me, trying to get away with Blayne and the bald vamp; the vamp dies, turning into black smoke.

When no one is looking, I put some dirt from Raven's grave in my pocket...

After Lana and Cricket stake the Vampires, I let them drive me back to my house in the car Raven bought for Cricket before school started. Neither one of them tells me I shouldn't be outside in the dark by myself, instead they just give me a lingering sideways glance. "I know," I say.

BLAYNE

Once we're sure we aren't being pursued by Shadows we stop running, arriving at a small-town store. Avy tells me he's not happy with me and not happy with being seen by the Hunter Lucas Kale. Avy makes sure we aren't in the view of any security cameras and the Leader of the Vampires smacks me so hard I land against the brick building. "Interact with them without my consent again and you'll see a different kind of Star." I was seeing all kinds of stars, but I knew what Avy Sinanna meant—God's star; the sun.

LUCAS

I know what I have to do. Inside the kitchen, I transfer the dirt I took from Raven's grave to a jar, and then I go to my room and get part of the Cypress Tree I brought back as a souvenir from one of the shops in South Carolina and put the items in a backpack. I've been doing research for the last couple of weeks. I lift up my mattress and pick up the summoning spell I got from the internet; I knew my cousin wanted Raven's diary and since he's a genius I didn't want to risk Leon figuring out the code to my safe just to get the diary and accidentally discover what I was up to.

I sling the backpack over my shoulder and head outside. Before I get in my truck Leon asks me if

I've seen Mozart. "No. Why?" I ask.

"I haven't seen him since yesterday morning and neither have the others."

"Don't worry. I'm sure he will turn up. He usually does." I say reassuringly.

Leon was really worried I could tell. I don't think Mozart had ever been gone this long… I don't have time for this though and I get in my truck and hurry down the driveway. I drive the dirt road past my neighbor's and soon I come to the middle of nowhere. A four-way where two dirt roads meet. There is absolutely nothing out here, not even a store nor a house. Just two roads and their signs.

I look at my watch. I'm five minutes early. At midnight it will officially be Halloween—the day of the dead…

~~~~

Chapter 12
Day of the Dead

October 30
The day before Halloween

HOME

I AWAKE FROM MY dream about Leon. I don't remember much of it, but I was in his bedroom. I feel super sick. This is the worst I have felt since being here; wherever this house or whatever is located. I don't think I've eaten real food since September. My eyes finally adjust to the dark; it's pitch black. I try to move my arms and legs but something is keeping them down. I realize I'm not laying on my blankets. I know I'm supposed to be panicking, but I'm not. I haven't yelled or said one word to my kidnappers. The door opens and I hear footsteps. The light clicks on, followed by the sound of dog feet...

The room suddenly becomes more illuminated than it has ever been; to my knowledge. It hurts my eyes and I squint from the fluorescents blinding them. I'm not used to this.

I don't know what day it is, but it feels like it's been a while since I last saw my dog, Leon, and Lucas. I have a feeling there won't be a rescue team coming for me, yet I don't feel the least bit worried. One of them slaps my face. I laugh and open my eyes. The blonde doesn't like this; me laughing. I can tell it bothers him. That song by Marilyn Manson plays again. Is that…Mozart? Is that my dog? No…something is… That four legged canine starts shifting… He suddenly becomes that red-headed kid.

I don't know what they expected from me, but I give absolutely no reaction to this. They have no idea whom they are messing with. They better kill me… I laugh again. I've lived decades and decades, a time when magic was at an all-time high; this little shapeshifting trick means nothing to me. However, them raping a young girl and kidnapping me means everything. And all though I don't know where Mozart is; the real one; I know he isn't hurt… I don't know how, but I know…

The red-head looks scared; as they all should be. The man though, his eyes and soul darker than his ugly scraggly facial hair, thinks he's going to break me. But he doesn't know what breaking is.

The man—all human, not a Shapeshifter—gets a knife. I know what his plan is—torture. He cuts my left arm. And I just stare at him while the song *Sweet Dreams* blasts through the basement. I lay there on his table. Waiting… I'm not sure what I'm waiting for but it's coming… And it's going to devour him. All of them.

The curly blonde cuts my right arm. I don't even

shed a tear. I'm gone and they can't even comprehend where. I doubt anyone can. I've traveled the world and its seven seas; they have no idea what pain is.

The man tells the sixteen year old, the red-head Mozart Shapeshifter, that it's his turn in the game. The man tells him to pick up the butcher knife. The kid doesn't want to play. But it's too late. He's been playing the cards. He was dealt a hand and he played. There is no forfeiting in the middle of a game. The kid takes one last glance at me and runs for the basement stairs. I don't know what happens because it's out of my view, but after the man leaves my sight I feel something wet land on my body. I know it's blood. Game Over. For him.

And then there were three of us; the teen boy my age, the thirty year old man who thinks he's something special, and the force stirring about inside this body. It wouldn't be much longer now… I couldn't help but smile.

Glasses—the curly-haired blonde boy—tells his stepfather I'm making him uncomfortable. He doesn't like the way I don't speak. And my previous stoicism, no reaction to the fake Mozart and them slicing my skin makes him extremely nervous. The man tells him to go play Mozart. The kid leaves and I sleep.

The time is closer…

Midnight
Officially Halloween morning

LUCAS

This is the place. I set my backpack down on the road where the two dirt roads meet. It's been a month since I saw Raven. Since the night the three of us went to get Halloween decorations.

I figured since Demons are real and magic exists again, and according to stories from before The Banish there used to be what others called a "Goddess at the crossroads with three forms". Back then I'm sure people thought of them as "gods", but I knew it was a Demon. And that there would one here, at the crossways—a place of great magic; usually bad.

I get the piece of Cypress Tree out from my backpack and lay it on the ground. I look around, feeling like someone might catch me. But there is nothing or no one out here; besides my truck. I do the incantation; my lips quickly moving. When I'm done reading the summoning spell out loud I wait. Nothing happens. Then I hear a noise behind me and I turn around. A doe is standing there, wide-eyed and staring at me. A light fog stirs around the two of us. It's happening just like the material I read earlier in the week said it would. I stand very still, waiting for the silver crossbow to appear, and when it does I slowly bend down and get it. The doe watches me as I cautiously stand upright and point the loaded crossbow. *Goddess with three forms.* The deer is one of the three forms of the goddess aka Demon, and killing the deer and mixing the blood and cypress together will release her into a human form; something I can communicate with on this plane of existence.

I hesitate for a second, but I can't stop now. I've come too far. I release the silver arrow. It connects with the doe, it falls over and blood pours out, and I hurry to it. I pull the arrow out and go back to the place where I laid the cypress. I get my backpack that still has the dirt and sling it over my shoulder and I toss the bloody arrow to the ground on top of the piece of Cypress Tree. I stand back, waiting. There's lightning, but no rain or thunder, and it seems to grow even darker out here beneath the sky. The fog turns red and a dark red cloud erupts from the bloody pile, and a woman in a red and silver gown appears directly across from me.

"Free at last," exclaims the woman, only I think she looks like a young woman in her late teens and taller than me. Not exactly what I was expecting. But looks are the least of my concerns right now. "I'm guessing you're the crossroads pimp, *Hecate?*"

"Hecate, Artemis; you kids change the meaning of words and names faster than a menopausal woman changing moods. Like the word 'gay' used to mean happy, now it stands for something entirely different. And the rainbow was a sign from God that he wouldn't destroy the Earth again with water and now—"

"—Yeah that's humans for ya. Listen, Princess,—" I feel my throat tightening, and it forces me to stop talking. I should have known her powers would extend beyond what was documented.

"Listen, *Prince Syphilis*. I'm not your little bitch. You came to me and you will do well to remember you're the little biotch. Got it, Lower Being?"

The pain in my throat subsides. "Yeah, okay," I say. "I don't recall having syphilis though."

"What do you want?" She clearly wants to get down to business, which is fine with me.

"Well, Hecate—"

"*Cynthia.* I prefer Cynthia. It's from my birthplace."

"Your birthplace? I thought Demons were Angels that fell from Heaven or something?"

"Mount Cynthus in Delos, a country in Heaven, yes. And what makes you think I'm a Demon? Why not an Angel?"

"I'm fairly certain an Angel wouldn't have tried to grind my larynx down for a bowl of soup."

"Maybe. Anyway, did you come here for a history lesson, midget?"

I'm offended, but I let it go. "I want you to raise someone from the dead." I get the jar of dirt from my bag and hand it to her. "My friend, Raven."

She laughs. "You want me to raise the former Goddess, dear Lucas?"

I'm taken aback. "How do you know my name and R—"

She points to herself— "higher being" —and then points at me— "little dude guy. You think just because we've been branded 'bad' we're idiots?" She points to herself again— "higher creature"— and then points at me— "Prince of syphilis."

"I've had it with the syphilis crap," I say and go to punch her. I hear a loud growl and something knocks me to the ground. I can't see what it is, but something sharp digs into my neck and it feels like I have a huge pile of bricks stacked on me.

"Not yet my pretty," she says, and then suddenly I see an angry and vicious dog big as a pony. Its teeth are the size of my head and I don't want to get caught in those babies. "My bad," I nervously laugh and hope she calls off this Hell Hound.

"So you came here to sell your soul to save someone you love? How very Winchester of you," she referenced a CW show about two brothers who would do anything for each other. "Uh, basically," I try to sound confident, but it's a little hard with a giant dog from Hell sitting on your chest with his claws ready to chop up dinner.

"Sit, Peaches." She calls it off and I feel the weight lift as it disappears. Probably going invisible again; I highly doubt it left. *She named it Peaches? Its breath didn't smell like no peaches,* I think to myself, getting up off the dirt road.

"Unfortunately, I can't do that. Even if I wanted to. I don't have the power to bring people back to life."

"But I read—"

"I once read that the Earth was flat. Sorry, honey. I can't grant you that wish, but I do have a lovely proposition for you. I'll give you Avy Sinanna." She definitely has my full attention. I've been searching since my childhood for the torturous Vampire who murdered my dad and aunt. "What's the price?" I ask.

"Convince your cousin to give up his visions, seeing the past."

"No way in hell."

"What has seeing the past done for you? Raven

was the only one with real gifts, *real* power, and now she's gone. Are you sure you don't want Avy? Seems like a waste; you looking for him and holding a grudge all those years. I can show you right now where you can find the Vampire."

"How do I know it's not a trick? I believe Demons are Demons for a reason."

"I can get one of those glorified Angels of yours here."

"You're just going to summon an Angel?" I ask with disbelief. "Your enemy? Don't they kill your kind?"

"Sweetie, —

"—NO, I'm not."

"Magic exists in the world now; it's the only reason you can see me, and nor Angel or Demon can fight in front of human sight. You would know how to kill us and we certainly don't want that. So with magic being around—again—finally; thanks to our wonderful Ray—"

"Don't you say her name like you were friends you evil—"

"—You treat me like trash, but yet you want my help. Humans. So dramatic."

The crossways Demon grabs my right shoulder and I yell when she stabs me in my left one. She yanks the knife out and we become separated by a reddish-black cloud. The cloud is thick, forcing me to cough into the fold of my arm. I've been hunting animals long enough to know the sound of an arrow being released from a bow, and I notice the weird fog starting to lift. Breathing becomes way easier; not like I'm breathing through a plastic bag anymore. I look down for the arrow and quickly find it. It's silver, like the one I used to kill the deer. But this arrow is way bigger, fitted for a very big bow.

"I'm the Angel of Truth," a male voice cuts through the disappearing fog. A naked masculine build creature without a penis creature strides over to me. His body is silver with gold and black markings, like tattoos, but I know they're not. The creature places his human looking but glowing hands on my bleeding knife wound. The knot in my stomach eases, the pain in my shoulder is gone, and the bleeding stops before I can even believe what I'm witnessing. I'm left with nothing but a cut.

The thing healed me so I just went with it. *He's an Angel. Fine. Whatever.*

"KILL HER," I nearly growl for the guy to end the Demon's life for knifing me. I realize at some point in time the moon must have come out. He bends over, picking up his arrow, and the light catches the bow over his shoulder. The bow and arrow have some type of wolf image and the initials P.A.

Silver and black wings flutter—like they're floating—behind the one referring to himself as the Angel of Truth. His hair is blonde like hers—the crossways Demon. They look like they could be twins...

"Calm down. Stabbing you was just so I could get him here," she nods. "And he couldn't kill me right now even if he wanted to." The evil crossways Demon reminds me. "Magic magic. Who's got the magic these days? So tiny human do you want to trade or not?"

"What do you want to show me?"

"I will show you were Avy is going to be at tomorrow. November First. He is guaranteed to be there if Leon gives me his visions. And you won't even have to leave the state."

"Is this true?" I ask the Angel who also looks like a teenager. "And why aren't your wings attached?"

"Yes. What my fallen sister says is true. And my wings are attached, you just can't see them because that's a sacred part to us. Humans are not worthy. Yet."

I thought about the creature Cynthia and her offer. Raven was indeed gone, and who better than Avy Sinanna to make suffer for everything bad in my life? "Show me."

"Bring Leon back here at eleven pm. Halloween night," she tells me after the vision ends.

I know where to find Avy Sinanna… If Leon gets rid of his power…

* * *

STATEN

October 31

HOME

Halloween

I had the strangest dream. That... Angel guy, I still haven't come to terms with their existence, but that guy was definitely starring in my dreams. I'm not exactly sure what happened.

"You okay?" Leon asks, putting plates of pancakes and bacon down in front of me. "I mean, I know what today is so I don't expect you to be Mr. Joe Sunshine."

"It's not entirely that. Weird dream," I confess, and he goes back to get the syrup.

"It's probably just the holiday," my cousin says over his shoulder, wearing his Halloween pajamas. I take some pancakes and a few pieces of bacon and put them on my plate. "Speaking of dreams," I start. "I read about the ones you had of Raven. Why didn't you mention it?"

"I guess I didn't think it was that important," he shrugs, sitting down. "I had one last night. It was super intense," he tells me with wide eyes. "For a moment I actually believed she was real, Lucas. I wasn't even asleep. I was awake, and I'm pretty sure I had a full blown hallucination, Luke."

"Okay, that's twice you've said my name. Clearly, you think you're going nuts. But chill-out, dude. Like you said—the holiday. I guarantee you won't have a single one after tonight."

"I hope so," he says chewing on a piece of

bacon. I think back to my own dream. That guy with the silver bow said *don't do it.* I think. Really the only thing I can clearly recall was the loud crowing noise. And went I woke up there was an actual crow outside my bedroom window. It was making so much noise that I got up to see what the heck was going on. When I opened the curtain it flew away from the Halloween graveyard. "So, what can you tell me about mythology?" I ask him.

"Everything..." his eyebrow raises skeptically. Mythology is only one of his favorite subjects.

"Was there ever a god with a silver bow with the initials P.A?"

Leon drops his fork and squints his blue eyes at me. "Are you high?"

"What? No. I just..." I trail off, feeling a confession coming on.

Mozart trots into the kitchen along with Leon's dog Roxy. "There he is!" Leon exclaims, overjoyed. "Where you been at buddy?!" He rubs Mozart behind the ears. He pets his dog and then gets up from the table and feeds them their dog food.

I finish my breakfast and put the plate in the dishwasher after I rinse it. We both have taken the day off and sometime after noon we decide to get out of our pajamas. Rachel, Lana, and Cricket should be here around six. The plan was to start the pumpkin carving when they arrived. The five of us planned on hanging out together, celebrating and honoring Raven's memory. I set my uncle up on a date; finally. Originally I was going to fix them up back in May, but the zombie thing interrupted my plans and then after that I just wasn't really thinking about it I guess. The lady is the mom of one of the guys who works for me; she's perfect for the ole' man.

After changing clothes, I go outside and help Leon. He wants to make sure the witches, ghosts, scarecrows, and everything are secure. "Why are we doing this?" I ask, checking the yellow caution tape on the fence that one of my cousins planted. "It's supposed to be a clear night."

"I don't know. I just… Raven. It's how I'm coping," he says, running his fingers through his long brown hair. "I just want things to be perfect." The fall wind blows, causing me to shiver. I look over and Mozart is sitting in the grass staring at me… I don't know why, but this kind of creeps me out. "You know, you haven't played with him at all since she died," Leon cuts in, interrupting our weird staring contest. "I don't know why," I admit as he calls the dog over. Leon asks the furry little fellow to shake and Mozart puts his paw in my cousin's hand. "I just can't," I say and walk back to the house.

Inside, the TV is playing a Halloween flick. I think back towards the first of the month when Leon and I watched HALLOWEENTOWN. The little girl's voice comes back to me; *someone's coming.*

Mozart comes in through the doggie door in the kitchen and I shut my bedroom door behind me. I feel bad; dodging him. But I have things to think about right now…

Halloween night

Before the others arrive, I decide to finally tell Leon about the argument I had with Raven. I don't know why I expected him to be upset because he wasn't; in fact, he hugged me and reassured me her death wasn't my fault.

We were in the kitchen and Mozart was in the living room; away from me when Leon asked if I had noticed anything strange with Roxy. "Honestly, dude, I haven't really been paying attention." "Eben said she's been hanging out over there a lot more than usual and I asked—"

"Wait. Eben actually spoke non-douchy words to you?"

"Yeah, talk about apocalypse time, right?"

I look around and I don't see his dog. "Is she over there right now?"

"Yeah. Rachel called me. I don't know what it could be…" He dumps a bag of candy into a plastic pumpkin. The candy is pretty much for us and the others; we've never had a trick-or-treater.

I don't know what to say about my adventure last night. I'm not entirely sure how I feel about it; trading my cousin's visions, which he hasn't had in a long time, just so there would be a guarantee on catching Avy Sinanna. The others will be here any minute now. I decide to drop the bomb; everything from me going to the crossroads to that crow crowing outside my window. Leon doesn't say much; just sits there bug-eyed and then asks me, "Are you sure you're not high?" I dismiss the question and tell him that ultimately the decision is his since he will be the one doing the sacrificing. And then there is a knock at the door. Our guests are here. "We have until eleven tonight," I remind him.

Before the pumpkin carving we all take a shot of liquor in Raven's name. I don't really care about doing the carving but I participate anyway; ripping the guts out made me a lot happier. Lana and Leon prepare the seeds for roasting; based on her mother's recipe. Afterwards, the others change into their costumes. I never planned on doing a costume; I'm not *that* much in the Halloween spirit. Rachel realizes she forgot her papers. Lana volunteers to go back with her and they get in Rachel's vehicle.

My phone rings. I answer. It's Pretty Boy. *What the heck does he want?*

Olsen talks so fast I'm not sure I'm understanding. He says something about him getting a new locator chip implanted in Mozart because the old one is about to expire. I didn't even know Mozart had one of those. Olsen tells me that when he got on his computer, to see if the chip was still working, the device showed Mozart about thirty miles from our house, and that he was calling because he thought something might have happened. I confirm that Mozart is right here in the living room. "I'm looking at him right now."

Then Olsen tells me to give Mozart a bowl of turnip greens and if that's the real Mozart he will eat them. *The real Mozart?*

I open the can of turnip greens and dump them in the dog bowl and take them to the canine in my living room. He sniffs at it and just stares up at me…

Cricket and Leon are staring me.

"Maybe he's not hungry," I tell Olsen.

"That's not Mozart," he says with absolute certainty. And my skin goes cold.

The dog's expression changes. He, she, it—whatever this thing is, understands what's going on. I drop the phone. The dog goes to run and I catch it before it can take off. It snaps at me, planning on biting me, but Cricket kicks it in the side. I think he heard the phone conversation. I'm still holding on to fake Mozart when the white and gray fur starts to disappear from my fingers. It turns into *skin.*

Someone I've never seen before stands uninvited in my house. *How long as this thing been living with us?*

The curly haired boy lunges for Leon's throat. I pick up my pistol that's always on the end table when I'm home, and take it off safety. I pull the trigger. The Shapeshifter hits the carpet and I put a bullet through his head. Kill first; ask questions later.

I pick the phone up off the floor. I'm about to ask Olsen for the real Mozart's location when there's a knock at the door... I know it's not the girls coming back...

* * *

I'm awake. I'm not sure when, but I know I've stopped receiving heavy medication. I've been awake for an hour. It feels like an hour. The small light is on, and I turn my head; the calendar tells me it's my holiday—the one I like so much.

HOME

I would try wiggling free from the straps that bind me to the table, but I know it's no use. I have no idea where my shapeshifting kidnappers are; one is dead, another is probably somewhere pretending to be my dog, for whatever reason, and the other is probably still close by.

I get the feeling he's still in the vicinity...

I'm awake but I'm extremely weak and I have lost all hope of Olsen and others rescuing me. But I know that somehow I will be released from this madness. I cling to the fact that I saw HIM. At least I think I did; my hunger state is really getting to me and my head feels super bad...

I've been wearing my red skirt this whole time and I'm surprised they haven't done to me what they did to Caitlin. I'm not sure what they are waiting for...

The door that leads down to the basement opens, and I get ready for another round. The sound of his big boots pounding down the stairs and echoing off the basement walls feels like a rhino stomping on my brain.

I hear him sharpening his tools and then something digs deep inside my leg. I almost scream but something stops me... My laughter makes him mad and he violently stabs my other thigh, right below my skirt.

I haven't eaten real food since they've taken me; I'm pretty sure they just feed me through tubes. I'm starving and there is no telling how much blood I lost yesterday during his game... If he keeps at it... Either someone will rescue me soon, or death will. Either way, it's coming...

The pain in my body hurts like hell, but I just keep on laughing. He smacks me in the face and I nearly see stars. I guess he undid my straps because I feel him sling me to the ground, and the wind gets knocked out of me.

It's coming...

Chains snap around my fragile wrist; tying me again to the brick wall, and my breath burns as it returns. I can barely understand the words he speaks to me. "Is that funny? I got a cure for that. Let's try something else." I hear his buckle rattle. His fingers squeeze my jaw and I open my eyes. His belt is undone and he says something about my mouth. I say something that really frightens him and his eyes grow wide like an animal about to be slaughtered.

I'm not sure what's happening...

One minute I'm in chains, the next minute I'm out of the basement and I'm upstairs standing in front of a cage... My Husky is clearly happy upon seeing my presence. I black out again, and the two of us are outside on the front porch. The white rose dangles by my side as the two of us begin the journey home; the moon and stars guiding the way.

Another blackout consumes me and when I come to Mozart and I are on the sidewalk in some neighborhood. Teenagers and a few adults dressed in costumes gawk at us, and a couple of kids drop their candy and stare. Someone tells me my costume is cool, and then I remember I'm covered in blood. We continue walking.

I'm very much dazed.

The gray and white dog trots ahead of me and stops at the end of the sidewalk and when I come near the end I stop beside the dog. I don't bother looking anywhere; I just stare at the sidewalk on the other side of the road. A car passes by us and then the dog takes off and I follow his lead.

At some point in time I realize my feet are aching and my entire body feels like... My eyes close and I feel myself sinking down to the concrete...

Now, I'm standing at the end of a very familiar driveway next to a mailbox holding my high heels in one hand and the bloody rose in the other...

I follow the dog as he leads the way. My vision is blurry. I'm not exactly sure what it is that I'm seeing up ahead in the yard. There are a bunch of lights blinking on off and changing patterns. My bare feet drudge through the cold grass and I begin to shiver.

We pause at the open gate; decorated with lights and other stuff I can't clearly make out. I think there was a gunshot from inside the house, but then again I'm not sure...

The dog, I think he's mine, continues on and I let him lead me through the maze in the yard and up to the porch. Some of the decorations start talking.

I stare at the door.

I'm not sure what to do. I feel like I've been here before. But I'm not sure where this place is or what's on the other side of this barrier. I knock...

After a moment, it slowly opens and three guys stand there—staring at me as if they've seen a ghost. I recognize them. "Lucas," I say barely above a whisper.

I'm safe now.

STATEN

I close my eyes and go to sleep.

~~~

Epilogue

BLAYNE VANDOR STANDS in the middle of the basement anxiously twirling the necklaces he took from Raven's friends after they died in Kansas; the unicorn from Ganesha and the red ruby from the Shadow; Sheba. "Raven's gone," the vamp says disappointedly, surveying the blood splattered on the floor and walls.

"I figured as much," Avy Sinanna says, stepping off the last step and onto the floor of the basement.

"Don't fret dears," their superior says delightfully, unexpectedly walking through the basement wall; without damaging it. And Blayne nearly jumps out of his skin.

"We have enough. You accomplished what you set out to do," Silhou praises and twirls around in her blue and silver cape. She turns to the young vamp. "And it turns out little Blayne here had a good idea." She glides past him and over to Avy.

The girl hands Avy Sinanna a disc. "See the highlights for yourself." Silhou smiles and starts up the basement stairs. "Happy Halloween!"

To be continued...

~~~

Thank you for reading my book. I hope you enjoyed it. Please take a moment to leave me a review. I can't wait to hear from you!
xoxo -*Angel*a

P.S. Look for

Home
REBIRTH,

the much anticipated sequel to *Home*.
~~

ABOUT THE AUTHOR

Angela Dawn Staten (March 1988) wrote her very first novel at an early age. She was just twenty-five when Blue Solace was published. This is her second novel in *The Blue Solace Series*. Angela was born in Georgia, and raised in Tennessee (USA). She was voted biggest bookworm by her classmates from Springfield High School (2006). Angela also has a background in modeling and acting.

**ALSO BY ANGELA DAWN STATEN
Blue Solace
*Check out my website for an updated list of books, interviews, and more!
https://angeladawnsworld.wordpress.com
Come say Hi on Facebook, Twitter, and Instagram!

CPSIA information can be obtained
at www.ICGtesting.com
Printed in the USA
BVOW04s1851140517
484112BV00001B/5/P